MIRYAM OF JUDAH

OF JUDAH
Witness in Truth & Tradition

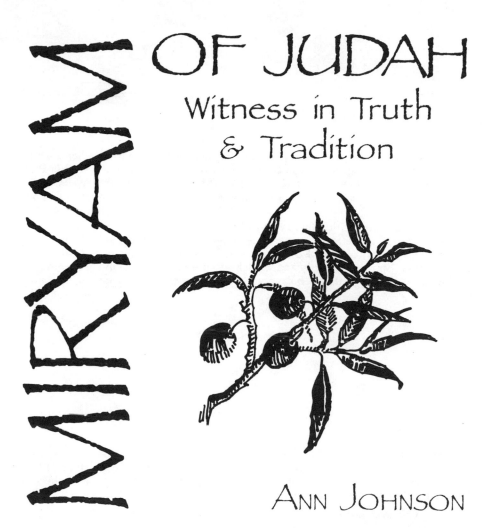

ANN JOHNSON

AVE MARIA PRESS ● **Notre Dame, IN 46556**

About the Author:

Ann Johnson makes her home in Weston, Vermont, where she focuses her attention on writing and teaching. She is the author of *Miryam of Nazareth* (Ave Maria Press, 1984) and the cassette tape *Stress and Spirituality* (Modern Cassette Library, 1986). The mother of five grown children, Johnson is a graduate of Northwestern University and Antioch College.

In 1985 she joined with Rabbi Perry Cohen in a partnership that engages them in a full schedule leading retreats, conferences, days of prayer and Sabbath and Seder liturgies. This activity is grounded in the prayer ritual and learning of the gospel community, whose "spiritual integrity and wholehearted commitment to living the covenant was based on the belief that a holy peace on earth is possible, is indeed the earth's destiny."

©1987 by Ave Maria Press

Library of Congress Catalog Card Number: 86-72638

International Standard Book Number: 0-87793-354-5
0-87793-355-3 (pbk.)

Cover and text design: Thomas Ringenberg

Printed and bound in the United States of America.

ACKNOWLEDGMENTS

Many deeds of kindness, many acts of graciousness season this book. Among them five leave lasting gratitude in my memory:

Blu Greenberg's loving book *On Women and Judaism* drew me into the faithful obedience of Jewish women in the niddah ritual, and her joy inspired the mikvah sections.

Rabbi Eugene Burowitz' lectures on the *Prayers of the Pharisees* nearly a decade ago at the Vermont Biblical Conference at Trinity College sparked a quest which manifests a few of its gifts here. Neither of these two scholars is aware of my work with their material. I hope I have done them honor.

Rabbi Perry Cohen has been a patient resource in my relentless forays into scripture. His willing consultation and thoughtful consideration have enriched this book. The idea for living the sabbath indicated in the gospels was his and I only wish you could share all the melodies he brings to his sabbath celebrations.

Josephine Hertz, friend of a friend of Rabbi Cohen, welcomed me into her London flat for tea on a brisk winter day and I was nourished in her sharing of precious memories. She is the daughter of Rabbi Joseph A. Hertz, Chief Rabbi of the British Empire for some 33 years which spanned wars and Holocaust, refugees cared for, European Jewry in agony. She served as his first lady after the death of her mother and was his assistant in his brilliant writing. Hertz' Siddur and Commentaries as well as the little treasure, *A Book of Jewish Thoughts*, were primary resources for this book and are a wealth of Judaism in its most open and sacred thinking, a gift for a student. She introduced me to Phineas May, curator of the Jewish museum, which is located on a site dedicated to her mother's memory and overflowing with living history lovingly remembered and delightfully shared by these two dear friends.

Frank Cunningham, editor at Ave Maria Press, was persistent in his belief that my research and my ramblings during our conversations would make this book another experience of Mary worth sharing with readers. His confidence and prodding led me where I was hesitant to go and I thank him most sincerely. It has been a joy-filled and emotional experience. My faith as a Christian is deepened immeasurably by embarking on the journey he made possible.

For Ezra

CONTENTS

INTRODUCTION

Christians look to one primary figure as the first witness of their faith. She is the model, the living testament of a human being's potential to change the world with a faithful "yes!". That figure is Mary—called in her time by her Hebrew name, Miryam. She lived in the village of Nazareth and was identified, as was her son, as a Nazarene. Thus Miryam of Nazareth was her customary designation.

Her faith life, precious in a deeply personal way, has become nourishment for many throughout the world, in numerous cultures and in different historical contexts. Far from the life she lived in Nazareth, her testimony is experienced within a larger arena, on a richly cosmic stage. Much of her vitality, however, reveals itself in the historical religious context of her life, which was rooted in ancient Israel. As Christians we gain insight into her wisdom, her God-centeredness, and her sacred task by coming to know her in the focus of her Judaism. This, then, is the purpose of this book—to invite us to cast our eyes upon her as a woman faithful in her Jewish religious observance . . . as Miryam of Judah.

The context of these reflections is the time from late morning Friday, the day of sabbath preparation—the day of the crucifixion—until the morning of the first day of the week, which we call resurrection morning. This is a precious time for Christians, a time held sacred and prayer-filled in our communal liturgy and private hearts. Who of us has not speculated, "What if I had been there walking with them?" Who of us has not knelt in waiting at the entrance of the tomb or stood watch at the foot of the cross? Who of us has not wept, raged, agonized, been resurrected?

It is tempting to project weakness and confusion into this time of trial. However, I have chosen to write of strength, of mental discipline, of all-persuasive commitment, of unwavering faith, of devotion to the Torah. As Jesus taught in Matthew, "I have come to fulfill the law, not to change it."

Miryam of Judah is divided into three parts, called *Lineage, Learning* and *Miryam's Sabbath.*

The first section, *Lineage,* remembers Miryam as she must have walked in those final hours with those who loved her son. It pictures her gaining strength for the hours ahead—as Jews are accustomed to doing—by recounting the faith stories of her ancestors. She remembers the lives of the four women listed in Matthew's genealogy:

Bathsheba, whose teachings to Solomon in his developing years he lovingly remembered in the Book of Proverbs. (Some legends say it was his gift to her on his wedding day.) Bathsheba, whose living of Torah saved the line of Davidic monarchy, whose integrity is pure, since like Sarah, she is declared blameless in the king's adulterous act. Bathsheba, who attracted David's love not by careless seduction but by her integrity of spirit as she performed her mikvah ritual.

Ruth, whose faithful "yes" was above and beyond her duty, who cast herself under the faithful shadow of Israel for protection, who performed the ritual in detail according to commands from Naomi even though she did not fully understand. Ruth, whose poverty as a refugee was evident as she harvested of the corner of the field. Ruth, who became a matriarch in Israel. Ruth is symbolic of much of Mary's life.

Rahab, who declared her faith though she had not seen. This would be the task of the members of the resurrection community and all who followed them. Rahab lives in the letters of Paul and of James as a model for non-Jewish followers of Jesus.

Tamar, the most ancient of the "mothers," the foremother of Jesus' final message to his followers in their adherence to the sacred, loving Law: "What you bind here on earth shall be bound in heaven and what you loose here on earth shall be loosed in heaven"(Mt 16:19).

Learning, the second section, explores Jesus' teachings as they might well have been understood and taught by the Jewish followers of that time. The community would carry these on and teach them to others in his name.

The teachings as expressed in *Miryam of Judah* are gathered from the rabbinical treasures of the times, coupled with understandings of loving traditional reflection and the needs of our times. You will note many familiar passages and thoughts from the gospels. You will, I'm sure, become acquainted with new lessons, turns of phrases, insights and images. Mary was a woman of rabbinic times. Hillel, Chief Rabbi of Jerusalem during the first half of her life, was the revered guide of her people until his death in approximately 10 C.E. (the Common Era—after the life of Jesus). There is speculation that this was the rabbinical school which attracted the young Jesus during his visit at age 12 to Jerusalem. After the death of Hillel a bitter political struggle between two pharisaic schools ensued. Ultimately the severely conservative school of Shammai was installed in Jerusalem, sending the disciples of Hillel into desert monasteries to live, teach, and remember his tradition. It is in the magnificent teachings of Hillel that we find the closest parallels to the gospel lessons. The school of Hillel was recalled to leadership at the end of the first century, and lives today as normative Judaism.

Mary's rabbis were Hillel and her son. In her home, as in every Jewish home, were sacred texts: the Pentateuch for learning and study; Psalms, the Prophets, and a collection of small scrolls including Esther and the Song of Solomon; usually Ruth, Lamentations and most probably Ecclesiastes. These latter ones were controversial books, historically "kept alive by the people" while questioned and even suppressed (except for Esther) by various canonical bodies. In every Jewish home, storytelling was the way of passing on tradition and of clarifying teachings so that each human moment might be made into a moment of God, holy on earth.

Rabbinics is a rich and vital tradition thriving today that was heavily drawn upon for this text. The stories belong to the Jewish tradition, generously lent for the healing of the world. I am grateful. Wherein I have not captured their loving essence, I am at fault, not they.

The stories in *Lineage* and the teachings in *Learning* are enwrapped, as in a shawl of prayer, in the ancient and beautiful Kaddish prayer.

The Kaddish is a vivid prayer form weaving its way through ancient Hebrew life into the present day. Modern-day Christians may be most familiar with the "Mourner's Kaddish" which has been used since the Middle Ages following the death of a loved one. Members of families and communities say the Kaddish each day for a year following a death. It is part of the rich cycle of mourning and healing rituals in the Jewish tradition.

The word "kaddish" derives from "kadosh," holy. It is a prayer of sanctification. The form I have used in *Miryam of Judah* is the "Kaddish d'Rabbanan" or the "Rabbis' Kaddish," the prayer to sanctify teachings. It expresses belief in the All-Knowing One whose desire it is that we live as we were created to live, in the image of God. Through learning, by the faithfulness of teachers, by becoming disciples, by repeating the lessons and living them in daily deeds of kindness (hesed), we sanctify God's place—both heaven and earth—making peace and harvesting God's abundant fruits. "Kaddish d'Rabbanan" celebrates that process. In a culture of oral learning we can imagine experiential and participatory learning. A core phrase is sung out by the rabbi:

> May God shine forth in our lives as we feed the poor
>> and the stranger,
>>> and let us say, Amen.

and the response from those listening is sung back to the teacher:

> May God shine forth in our lives as we feed the poor
>> and the stranger forever and ever,
>>> and let us say, Amen.

The response formula "forever and ever" has strong historical roots in oral teaching.

And the "Amen" is crucial. "Amen! I believe! Yes! That is true! So may it be done!" Teaching actively engaged the people's voices, minds and hearts. "Amen! As you say so it is! In our lives so let truth be done! Alleluia! And let us say, Amen."

Jewish prayer books today capture that emphasis on active response in their reminder that whenever or wherever Kaddish is being said, all who hear stop what they are doing, listen and say "Amen."

The prayer dear to Christians, called "The Lord's Prayer" or the "Our Father," bears strong ties to a "Kaddish d'Rabbanan." The structure: 1) a speaking of the Name and hallowing it with gratefulness for creation and yearning for the joining of heaven and earth, 2) commitment to the preceding lessons, as in the Sermon on the Mount, 3) a prayer for peace.

The Kaddish prayer form may not be too familiar to Christians, but it is truly a prayer form of the times of the Jesus community. The teachings are so very precious. We today are urgently in need of understanding and living, hearing and doing the teachings of Torah as embodied in Jesus' words. I hope by re-speaking the covenant lessons and cradling them within the beautiful Kaddish prayer where they are accustomed to resting, we can live them out more faithfully.

The third section of the book is *Miryam's Sabbath*. According to historical records of the Hebrew liturgy, it is an accurate re-visioning of a sabbath the Jewish community would have observed. Many of the prayers were the harvest of the Ezra/Nehemiah period, the work of the elders of the Great Assembly. Some prayers like the Shema grew out of the desert experience recorded in Exodus. All the prayers are prayed today by faithful Jews. All the prayers seasoned the life and teachings of the resurrection community and live in the book of Acts and the letters of Paul, James and Peter.

The sabbath is a holy day, the day in which the world to come is lived on earth. What a challenge of obedience for this community, and yet every gospel tells us their activities on that day were observant of the Law. What a gift this day, with its healing words, peaceful rituals and sustaining memories must have been for them. The sabbath in the time of Jesus was truly a revolutionary event. A people who did not work one day a week, who invited the poor and the stranger to their family table, who laughed together, sang and danced, who befriended each other as God had befriended each of them made this day into an observable event for the environment in which they lived. So attractive was their joy that they often called undesirable attention to themselves. Local governments were not always pleased. Leaders often tried to suppress the spontaneous neighborliness. Strangers looked with longing upon this happy people and often wanted to convert. Jews in later years who were converting to Christianity often refused to leave the sabbath behind, and it became a problem between Christians and Jews. Until the sixth century converting Christians took two sets of vows: one declaring Jesus their Lord, and the other pledging never to celebrate the sabbath or other Jewish festivals. Jews were pressured to restrain their ritual from public eye and in some cases not permitted to celebrate. They quietly took the sabbath celebrations behind the closed doors of their homes to preserve them.

It is said that history is written from the perspective of the winners. Perhaps survivors is a less value-laden word. So, too, the faith practices of the Jesus community that have survived have been preserved in the Pauline letters and constitute the practices of Christianity today. They are primarily the practices reflecting the converts of the Greco-Roman world. The rise of Christian influence and power and the active conversion practices of Christianity wrought changes during the first five centuries of the Common Era which obscured for centuries the vitality of Judaism as it was lived by the gospel community.

The struggle of Jewish factions during the gospel period, as they sought to survive and hallow their practice in a Hellenized world, would be interpreted in the most negative light by Christians seeking to make their own place in a fragile faith environment. These interpretations are still read and preached today and have caused grief to the people of God, both Christian and Jew. From the time of Jesus, through the Holocaust and into the present day, the struggle to heal these wounds goes on.

Mary, mother of the Lord, was not part of the Hellenized community. From the writings in the gospels, the Acts and the letter of James, called brother of the Lord, we are given insight into the faith practices of the Jewish followers of the Nazarene rabbi. They remained faithful to the Jewish way, living the way of their Master within the heart of Judaism. Note the grace after meals prayer from David and Solomon. It details the work of the house church communities described in the Acts of the Apostles.

The destruction of Jerusalem in 70 C.E. was a tragedy of immeasurable proportions for the Jesus sect. Hellenistic reluctance to embrace the "narrow way" of the chosen people limited the appeal of the Jesus community, and converts embraced the more worldly ways of the Greeks and Romans. These simple Jews, people who never performed an act without thoughtfulness and prayer, are the family, the teachers and the consecrators of Jesus, our Lord. Let us experience one vision of them with respect and consideration for the gift their lives have been for us.

Ann Johnson

ORIENTATIONS

Some Hebrew words and rituals referred to in the book may be unfamiliar to Christians. Perhaps a word or two of explanation will be helpful.

YHWH: the Tetragrammaton, four letters which indicate the indescribably holy Name of God. YHWH is used 5,410 times in the Hebrew Bible and numerous other times in combination with descriptive names. It is commonly translated as "Lord" or, in Hebrew, as "*Adonai.*" Verbal utterance of the name YHWH shrank from use during the exile so that the Name would not be misused by antagonists. During the years of the Second Temple, the time of the gospel community, the Name was pronounced at certain times when the people were alone at prayer or in the Temple together at services. The pronunciation of the Tetragrammaton was known not only in Jewish circles but also in non-Jewish circles centuries after the destruction of the Temple.

YHWH is rooted in the verb form of "to be." Evolving interpretations of ancient script add meanings such as "One who calls into life," "Creator," "Maker of time and history," One who sends down," "the Breather." The two symbols, YH and WH, represent equal qualities of opposites brought together in perfect balance: mercy and justice perfectly resolved, masculine and feminine perfectly in harmony, rest and creativity, repentance and joy, evening and morning . . . all opposites perfectly united. The prayer for unification of the Name of God is still used in certain Jewish morning liturgy.

YHWH is a precious symbol. I leave to the reader the choice of how to speak the Name. Many Christians follow the *Jerusalem Bible* and use the word *Yahweh.* In some traditions *Jehovah* is accepted. The Jews place the word *Hashem* (the Name) in place of this Name which must never be carelessly used. When I am praying or reading silently I often simply pause, leaving the space filled with quiet listening and respect.

Shofar: the ancient ritual horn of Israel. According to the scriptures, it was this clarion that sounded forth from Mount Sinai to summon the people of Israel to their spiritual awakening in the Holy Law.

The construction of the horn varies: the ram's horn for Rosh Ha'shanna (new year and redemption) to represent the bent penitent; the long, straight horn of the wild goat for festivals. The *shofar* is never painted; it is carved to retain its ancient beauty. Its two notes vary in rhythm, combination and repetition according to the nature of the summons. The horn's melodies are well-known in Jewry; like the call of God's "voice," there is no mistaking its message.

The horn played an important role in preparing for sabbath. On Friday afternoon calls were blown at intervals: At the first, travelers on the road or the laborers in the fields ceased their work. At the second, the shops closed and city labor ceased. The third was a signal to kindle the sabbath lights at the home altars, the family dinner tables. Then, after a pause which allowed for the family rituals to take place, a fourth call was sounded consisting of a repetition of the previous three, and the sabbath had begun.

Mikvah: literally "a place of collection of natural waters or a pool made by a gathering of flowing natural waters (rain, underground spring or snow)," *mikvah* is a ritual prescribed for times of spiritual change of status or change of function of life often expressed as change from "unclean" to "clean." Clear directions are given regarding preparation of mind and body for this spiritual cleansing which has been part of Hebrew ritual observance since early biblical times. *Mikvah* appears in the gospels in the stories of John the Baptizer, and again in the Essene documents.

Quite remarkable archeological finds in the Holy Land have uncovered remains of the *mikvah* at the Mount of Olives with its divided pool for men and women and its system of clay pipes feeding fresh flowing spring water in and drawing it out in continual refreshment. The preparation and drying rooms, possibly open-roofed to provide a natural ceiling of leafy green and expansive sky, are still traceable in the ruins. The carefully hand-hewn stones of the floors, walls, pool and stairway are use-polished, exemplifying the love of a people for its religious treasures.

Two scenes of *mikvah* appear in this text: One is in the Bathsheba story at the occasion of her *niddah* or change from quiet physical care for herself to a return to communal and family life; the other, the ritual bathing in preparation for the sabbath to wash away the cares of the week, to enter the holy rest, to create a heaven on earth, a change from the six days to the one.

For the crucifixion community the *mikvah* would also have had the quality of washing away spiritual violence from their souls, cleansing their spiritual hands from the handling of death that they might turn and embrace life again.

Hesed: kindness. Of all the Judaic concepts which have been incorporated in this text, by far the strongest is the concept of kindness, *hesed*. *Hesed*, which is manifested in both the Hebrew and Christian testaments, is the one single idea with the greatest potential for healing, for understanding, for nurturing a broken and aching world, and for welcoming the poor and the stranger. Loving kindness, *hesed*, flows from God to God's beloved creatures, and is commanded by God between all people, one to another. *Hesed* is the sanctifying deed, the Law in whose presence all other laws stand aside, the way in which the holy and the human recognize each other. *Hesed* is detailed explicitly in Torah teachings regarding neighbors, parents, enemy, widow and child, stranger and the poor.

Sha'chein: neighbor, but a neighbor of special circumstance. It is not the usual neighbor, *ray'ah*, which means one who lives next to you. Who is my neighbor, my *sha'chein*? Jesus answers with the beautiful Samaritan story. Hillel answers by saying, "Your neighbors were with you in Egypt." Both indicate difficult situations where oppression, years of conflict and built-up antagonism might be found. However, in Egypt the Hebrew women are directed to go to their neighbors (*sha'chein*) with whom they share favor and respect to secure from them valuables with which to adorn their children and eventually build the religious treasure of the new Israel. "Thus did they save their neighbors in Egypt." (J. Hertz states that "save" is the only correct translation, though most of our bibles say "plunder" or "spoil" or "strip." Of the 212 times the word is used, he states, in 210 instances it means not to plunder but to "snatch from danger.") Again, as the Hebrews prepare for the tragic night of the angel of death, they are directed to slaughter a lamb which must be consumed by the gathered family in one meal. If the family is too small to consume it in one feast, they are to bring in their *sha'chein* to feast with them and thereby also be protected. Since few families could consume a whole lamb, there was plenty of protection for the Egyptian neighbors who had befriended the Hebrews in their oppression, with whom favor and respect were shared, and who were financing the beginnings of the new Israel. Indeed, neighbors precious as the indwelling of God were found in Egypt and were embodied in the Samaritan along the Jericho road. Holy neighborhood built in the midst of the oppressors' might is held precious and redeemed in the history of God's people.

Torah: the Law. Law and the struggle of the people of Israel to live it, discerning its meaning in each time and circumstance, make up the better part of the Hebrew scriptures. The oral Law stands equal with the written Law. The Kaddish reflects the understanding that each person who lives Torah "carries it along," enriching the name of God by the quality and the integrity of living, by teaching, and by example to others of the loving Law of God. People also have the power to diminish the Law by their lack of integrity. Torah seems to be life itself lived in the presence of God.

Shema: the primary prayer from desert time which all Israel sings twice a day declaring its faith. *Shema*, "listen," is the beloved central prayer of Jewry sung in the evening and in the morning, sung in the desert and in the cities, sung by Jesus. The song sung when the world was full of idols and frivolous gods, *Shema* declared Israel's God to be One Alone: "Hear, O Israel, YHWH is your God, YHWH Alone." In later years after the onset of Christianity, when the doctrine of the Trinity seemed to split the nature of God asunder and the precious Name could no longer be uttered, the understanding of the Hebrew came to be as it is today, "Hear, O Israel, the Lord your God, the Lord is One."

Nishmat: a sabbath prayer. The beautiful *Nishmat* prayer is used as the sample of sabbath morning communal prayer in this manuscript. *Nishmat* means "the breath," "the life of the soul in God." This *Nishmat* song is still sung in sabbath and festival liturgies. Strains echo from the desert: thanksgiving for rain, and not just for rain but for every drop of rain; for wonders and not just for wonders but for every wonder told in detail to friends and family, living on in the joy of sabbath conversation. Much to my amazement and delight, I found in the Rabbi J. A. Hertz' Siddur (prayer book) the reference to a recurring legend that the composition of the *Nishmat* prayer was traced to the pen of Simon Peter, one of the elders of the Jewish sect following the teaching of the Rabbi Jeshua ben Joseph of Nazareth, known in the Greek world as Jesus. The prayer is said to have arisen during the struggle of this community with Hellenism, as it clung to its beloved Judaic beliefs, prayers and practices. Legend or no, it gave me a new Peter: prayerful, brilliant, loving, mystical, mature and strong in his faith.

Selecting meaningful language for the disciple, the follower, as well as for the Name of God is a tender and a sacred task. I have designed a word which is expressive for me of the fullness of masculine and feminine qualities of God and likewise the faithful follower. That word is "genderful." I have also used three words that I would like to clarify: *handmaid, master* and *Lord.*

Handmaid is an irreplaceable name for the faithful follower. No other word so expresses the attentive fidelity, the pouring out of care, the tender love of one who desires passionately to serve God, to wait upon the Beloved One. Though seen in the feminine, the substance of the meaning is genderful. All of us are gathered into this one word, handmaids all of us who are held in the palm of God's hand.

Lord and *master*, both terms I regret have acquired painful shadows, have been co-opted in feudal times and oppressive situations. They are often relegated to the masculine although neither is masculine generically. Neither has a feminine equivalent. Both are rooted in genderful concepts. I trust we can reclaim them lovingly and return them to their traditional home in biblical language.

Lord is a translation of the Hebrew *Adonai*, fully feminine and fully masculine. *Adonai*, Lord, wellspring of my inner resources, governor of my inner urges. *Adonai*, Lord who gave me birth, who knelt kneading me from earth substance, who kissed into me the breath of life (*nishmat*). *Adonai*, Lord, caretaker of my personality and emotions. The cosmic equivalent of *Adonai* is *Eloheinu*, God, sovereign of the universe, the before and after, the grain of sand and the starry firmament, in the beginning, now and for everlasting unto everlasting.

Master is the one who knows, who understands, who perceives questions and gives the gift of answers to those who listen, the wise, the skilled, an original from which copies can be made, mentor, scholar, best friend (as one who has mastered the loving of another), beloved teacher, omniscient, source of wonders, giver of words. The one worthy to be called Master is one engaged in all of life, mind/body, female/male, child/adult, heaven/earth, bring together in wisdom (mastery) all opposites, harmonizing all evolution. The true Master is filled to overflowing with all the qualities of womanhood and manhood.

I'm aware of the longing for textual references throughout the book. Where fitting, they are inserted. Many sections which may seem strikingly recognizable are in fact combination prayers or synthesized passages. For instance, the Havdalah prayer ending the sabbath as adapted from the Jewish Siddur draws upon and weaves together the following: Isaiah 12:2-3, Psalm 3:9, Psalm 46:12; Esther 8:16 and Psalm 116:13. Words usually translated from the very lively and flexible Hebrew are especially shaped to reflect the contextual setting of the prayer; therefore, you may not recognize the references when you look them up in your particular bible translation. God's word lives in the mouth and speech most lovingly. In this spirit most of the scriptural references here are of my own adaptation from a multitude of translations and commentaries with an intent on deeper meaning enhanced by loving familiarity.

PROLOGUE

I am Miryam of Judah
    from yearning soul of Judah born;
    indeed, from Judah's pulsing heart brought forth.

Age upon age I journey,
    spilling sacred psalmody on Negev's sands.
Age upon age I journey,
    spending my sanctifying labor upon this fruitful earth.
Age upon age I journey,
    stilling human minds to receive a holy word.

I journey age upon age
    to gift with blessing this people
        hallowed and hallowing;
    to gift with blessing this material envelope we call living,
        in which the heart of God is tucked.

I am God's creature, eternal and defined.
Like each and all of us
    created,
    continually
    companioned.
Chosen to image God according to one particular pathway.

Upon three foundation stones does my world rest:
    upon God's Word . . . Law . . . Torah,
    upon God's service . . . prayer . . . tefilin,
    upon God's work . . . kindness . . . hesed.

Once I walked earth's soil in earthly time,
    beating stony miles with sandled feet,
    loving, learning,
    establishing my moment
        in the annals of shalom.
It is of that time I speak with you today.

Journeyer, it's time we renewed ourselves.
Once we stood together at a bend in time,
    but only for a moment.

There is pain in our past.
But today I will look forward in hope
    as Jews are commanded to do;
    let us begin again.
Let me tell you who I am and then perhaps
    you will speak yourself to me,
    reaching always for the best in both of us,
    for it is in our sacred dreams, our lifted vision of ourselves in God,
    that rests the hope of walking once again, together.

I journey as a Jew of Judah's clan:
    as one called forth from familiarity to ground myself in God,
    as one called forth from the security of bondage,
    as one summoned into the wilderness of unslavery.
    Escaped! Delivered to the raging freedom of maturity.
    Responding once to the love of God,
        I am now and forever responsible.
    Like one who does not halt between,
        I cast my lot with the still, small Voice.

I am one touched in the desert by YHWH.
    There I became one people,
        instructed in the loving Law,
            which, seeded in that holy time,

bears fruit in my life
and in the life of each one who embraces it.

I became Torah.
Well of God, revealed not in form but in ferment.
Law ever stable, ever changing.
I hearken to a still flaming bush
never consumed,
from whose root the Name is spoken.
With promises sweet I bound myself to God.
No other vow so sacred.
No other vow supreme.

I am called to Torah:
history and future, Torah-bound,
in frequent prayer and fervent learning,
in ritual remembering and kindly deeds.
Creation continued.
Thus I am instructed; thus I live.
Thus I am eternally grateful.

Called to be Jeshururn, the upright ones.
Called to be a clear-sighted people.
Cleansed in covenanted waters,
I dedicate myself to God.
I wrap myself in Torah,
vine begetting vine.
What I do on earth so is it done in heaven.

Chosen to be called Israel, the one who strives with God.
Named by YHWH, I am "holy priest," God's celebrant.
Named "wife."
Named "son" and "heir" and "daughter."
Named "light to the nations," named even
"a particular treasure."

I am image of God as are you and as are all who
        so specify their lives
            in order to reflect that One.
God's restive creation in all its ripe diversity.

I am Lion of Judah, pacing the earth in survey
        of my Torah-pride.
I am lamb of YHWH, nestled in a shepherd's arms,
        frolicking beside the lively waters,
        ripped and bloodied prey of driven predators.
I am bear burrowed deep and long in secret nurturing,
        bear in belicose defense of these, thy little ones.
I am turtledove cooing soft, oft-repeated melodies:
        cantoring in the land.
I am creature of ample wing, sheltering
        neighbor and stranger,
        mourner and child.
I am fig tree and olive,
        sweet oil, kind branch.
I am stuff of the earth,
        rose bud and garlic,
        rough stone and dust.
I thrive in simple work that multiplies,
        that increases, blessed by my prayer.
In my palms water, earth, wool, forge, lathe, and pen,
        fruit of the vine and bread for the day, become holy.

Always in my mind a pondered Torah-word . . . spoken, learned, lived;
        in my mouth a prayer of blessing, kind words to neighbor, friend;
        in my hand generous sustenance for the poor and stranger,
            the left one and her child;
        on my fingertips the blushed cheek of my beloved.

As I hold
        so am I held.

As generous as I am so will God be with me.

I am asked to spend my life in learning.
    I am single-minded.
    Some name it obedient, even legalistic.
    I name it faithful.
    I name it fiercely faithful.
With loving deeds and learning, I build a fence around the Torah,
    enclosing thereby a soft, protected, fertile place
        for God and I and all creation,
        thus to thrive and grow.
I make of my bodily life a fruitful paradise,
    sanctifying earth in all I do.

As one betrothed of God,
    I am one known.
    There is no part of me unknown by God.
    Our living vow to one another—Torah.
    Torah our abode.
Abiding there I knead my moments,
    ingredient of me kneaded in the grain of God,
        spirit-risen,
        life-baked brown,
    warm, sweet bread in the mouth of the world.
Abiding there I am provider:
    my work, my actions
        bring home this day to each and all
        abundance of God's provender;
    in my life, I can exemplify to others God's holy providence.
Abiding there with Torah, God abides with me
    and day by day I struggle,
    stiffened here, gentled there,
    bound to the timed and timeless Law by the tether of my heart,
    called only to hallow the Holy Name on earth,
        for as we do on earth so is it done in heaven.

History is our hope.
      God our intent.
      The world is our responsibility.
We tell the story with our lives speaking what has gone before
      and what is now.

We are responsive to all that has been,
      responsible for what will be.
      Responding, we construct new stories in our time.
We are a people not commissioned to preserve,
      but to remember;
      not held in rigidity, but faithfulness.
We are a living legacy of human wholeness
      rooted in the grasp of the divine.

Journeyer, is not now the time to travel,
      to stand heart to heart as once we stood within a bend of time?
I will begin and speak myself to you and listen,
      reaching always for the best in both of us,
      for it is in our sacred dreams,
      our lifted vision of ourselves in God,
      that rests the journey home.

I am Miryam of Judah.
Today I walk Judean hills again,
      this time with you,
      reliving my earth-moment.
Clasped in the fervor of covenantal devotion,
      filling full our covenantal cup
      to nourish searching persons then and yet to come,
      to sanctify time, humanity and earth.

PART ONE: LINEAGE

YHWH, I come.

Walking the Jerusalem road this spring day with others
    accompanying my beloved son,
      I fill the hours with rememberings.

YHWH, many are we here,
    walking this Jerusalem road.
    Many are we who have come to love him.
    We journey together like the gathered exiles
      summoned by God's shofar.

Sturdy, he is . . .
    sturdy of faith and heritage.

In Josef, he is of the line of the shepherd king,
    from Bathsheba and David sprung.
Of course, he resembles David . . .
    the singing, no matter the hour of prayer or the occasion,
      the everpresent song,
    the arm-in-arming with companions,
    the regal demeanor exuding an astonishing authority.
He is heir of David's house in blood and bone.

And yet, it is Bathsheba that I warm to.
Bathsheba's magnetic depth that draws me in his eyes.
Bathsheba remembered as the life-long, loving wife of David,
    respected of Nathan, the prophet,
    wise mother of Solomon,
    queen mother of Israel.

BATHSHEBA, WOMAN OBSERVANT AND WISE

Her Story...

2 Samuel 11:2—12:25
1 Kings 1:11—2:12

Bathsheba, married to a Hittite man, Uriah by name,
    daughter of Eliam (God is gracious), faithful Jew,
    held to the ways of Judah.

Bathsheba, bathing in ritual obedience on a Jerusalem roof,
    washed her body fresh returned from woman's flow
      in rain water collected there,
        cleansed herself as is required by our kindly Law.

It is this memory that conveys the loveliness and dignity
    in observing the sanctifying way.

She like I, a woman in Israel.
In days at the time of blood flow
    we are daughters of miracle.
    Separated, we are separate indeed.
      Like all women everywhere,
        bleeding from the core, we do not die.
        Womb-tides pull and ebb
        with the pulse of the universe,
        and we survive.
Protected in Israel, as in no other place
      by the mysterious Law, we thrive.

Hardy, the women of our cult,
        clean with the health of respect,
        clean in the constant attending to wisdom,
        clean because of the care of our God.

Touch me not!
    I am in the clutches of wonder.
Neither shall you fear me.
      There is no thing in my body that lies.

I distance myself from the busyness of others
      and attend to the vitality of flesh.
    Spirits pressed deep,
      thoughts turned inward,
        I rest.
    This is a sacred time.
In quiet confidence I spend these seven gentle days,
      vulnerable, sensitive, aware.

In a place removed, I gaze attuned with genuine affection
    upon my home and kin,
      seeing the precious things
        I am too close to see at other times.
Deep is the contentment in this mysterious law of God.

As the vine renews itself
    so am I renewed.
Immersed in the lively waters,
    purified.
Washed in a loving tradition,
    rededicated in God's design.

Woman in Israel, emerge from the waters embracing life.

Be eager for reunion,
      fertile and vibrant,
            healthy and cleansed.

Blessed are you, our God, Wise One everlasting
      who has called us to be holy,
            who has taught us to immerse ourselves in the lively waters,
            who has given us instruction to cleanse body and soul. Amen.

The body you have given is pure.
The law you have given is kind.
The love you have given surpasses understanding.

Bathsheba emerges centered, serene and vibrant,
      prayer-filled with ritual praises,
            tending her heritage, lifting her song.

On her roof-garden she reveled in Judah's refreshment.
From his roof the king watched,
      drawn deeply to her in a passion that would last a lifetime.
In her health and in her faithful love of God
      she was beautiful to look upon.
Bathsheba, daughter of Eliam (God is gracious),
      of the faithful family of Israel,
            Uriah's lovely lamb, his treasure,
            now beheld by David.
One glance at her ritual,
      casting his lot with her,
            David joined to her.
One step sealing them both into eternity.

The king had wived of the women of Hebron
      before establishing his house in Jerusalem.
      A woman of Israel he had never wived.

The king enjoined his cultic privilege and
     Bathsheba, like Sarah, blameless,
     lay within the king's purvey.

Never again would their stories be separate.
Never again Israel's song the same.

Their love consumated . . . what pain and cost to both of them
     we can only speculate.
The ancient scripture vibrates with their cries.
"David, I am with child."
And his protection offered for her name:
     a noble effort to secure appearance of Uriah's parentage,
       all to no avail, in desperation, finally,
     a warrior husband betrayed,
       conspired against even unto death.
Bathsheba's lamentations sounding as she mourned him.
For David, a prophet-condemning parable.
For David, an agony admitting his iniquitous act.
David stood before God, crying.
     His anguish echoes in our tents today.

     Be merciful to me, O gracious God,
       wipe out my offense.

       Wash me clean of my fault.
       Cleanse me from my sin.

     I give words to my unfaithful deed;
       my sin is always before me.

       Wash me clean.
       Cleanse me from this darkness.

It is you against whom I have acted.

You alone have I betrayed.

Wash me.
Cleanse me to cleanness again.

Create in me a clean heart, O God.
Renew within me a steadfast spirit.

Cast me not away from your comforting.
Take not thy holy spirit from my listening.
Give me back the joy of your saving presence.
Return the sustaining strength
        of a free and willing spirit within me.

I will teach others to make their way toward you.
Those who have turned away will return to you
        when they hear my story.

Free me from the guilt of the blood I have spilt;
        then shall my tongue revel in your justice,
        then from my throat shall pour forth
            proclamations of your mercy.

O Lord, open thou my lips,
        and my mouth shall show forth your praise.

You are not satisfied with the usual sacrifices.
Should I offer only a ritual empty of heart
        you would not accept it.
My sacrifice, O God,
        is my spirit, bent,
        my heart, broken.
My heart crushed and grieving, O God,
        you will not refuse.

With generous forgiveness did God season Israel.
From David and Bathsheba's grievous union
    a child was born.
As though responding to their agony,
    the child failed quickly.
David spent himself in prayer and fasting;
    nonetheless, the child died.
She mourned desperately and David went to her.
His lament as the child slipped away to death:
    O God, I shall go to him,
        but never again shall he come to me.
David stayed near to Bathsheba during her consolation.
He went to her and lay with her.

She conceived and they gave birth to a son.
She named him Solomon.
YHWH loved Solomon and
    made this known through the prophet Nathan.

Nathan regarded the child Solomon and named him with a holy name:
    named him Jedidiah, "beloved of YHWH,"
    in accordance with the desire of the Lord,
    which had been made known to him.

Solomon, beloved child,
    raised up by Bathsheba in wisdom and favor,
  Heir of Israel's sovereignty
    by virtue of promise alone,
  Builder of David's dream,
    a temple in Jerusalem,
  Fulfillment of Nathan's trust,
    a gentle man of prayer,
  Beneficiary of Bathesheba's teaching,
    wise judge of open access,
    sayer of compassionate sayings,

image of YHWH, merciful and just.
Solomon remained faithful to his mentors,
      mother, mother and prophet, mother and king,
      singing their praises, keeping their counsel,
      honoring their presence all his life long.

Bathsheba and David continued constant.
Other sons they bore named Nathan, Shobab, and Shimea.
David's reign in Jerusalem was thirty years.
At his dying time,
      sons, born earlier in Hebron,
         vied for kingship.
Nathan came to Bathsheba saying,
      Have you not heard,
      Adonijah, David's eldest, has established reign and
      David our anointed one knows it not?
      Now come, let us take counsel together.
      Let us avoid bloodshed and betrayal.
      Go thee unto David and recall to him his covenant
         with thyself, thy son, and this prophet.
      Behold, I will come also after thee and confirm thy words.
And so it was Bathsheba went unto David in his chamber.
Now he was aged and ministered to by Abishag the Shunammite.
Bathsheba gave David the honor due a vital sovereign,
      and David responded to her address.

She summoned his memory to their covenant and advised him at length
      on the course of events.
      As she spoke, it was announced by the king's advisors
         according to their arrangement:
      "Behold, Nathan the prophet."
      When he came in, Nathan confirmed her consultation.
      David responded, "Call again Bathsheba."
As she stood in his presence,
      the king renewed his covenant with her regarding Solomon
      and the governance of Israel.

She heard him out and blessed him:
        "Let David the sovereign of Israel, live in You forever," she prayed.

And they went out, Bathsheba, the prophet Nathan, and Zadok the priest, and while many rejoiced, they led Solomon riding upon King David's mule to the holy place of Gihon. In the presence of the people of Zadok, the priest took the horn of oil out of the tent and anointed Solomon.
And they sounded the shofar.
Indeed, the blowing of the ram's horn rang in the land.

All the people singing, "Long live Solomon."
All the people piping "Hoshanas," rejoicing.
All the people following in such gaity that the hills resounded and
        the earth shook with their dancing,
        the earth rent with the sounds of them.

Adonijah, who had established reign without David's consent,
        heard the festivity and knew its portent.
He sought sanctuary, grasping the horn upon the altar.
But Solomon, beloved of God,
        child of Bathsheba who had raised him up in the way of God,
        Solomon imaged God in his judgments.
        He called forth decency from Adonijah and
                commissioned him mercifully,
                "Go in peace to thy own house."

David's life drew to a close.
He charged Solomon to be a man of God.
David died, joining his ancestors.

Solomon reigned in wisdom.
Nathan the prophet continued in his trust.
Bathsheba, queen mother, sat often at his right hand.

Solomon loved her and honored her.

Kaddish of Remembering

YHWH in the gift of Bathsheba's story,
     I know your intent for us more deeply.
Hearken to my Kaddish of remembering.
Teach me, O God.
In the lives of those who love you
     I come to know your love.

Great and holy is your name, O God,
     revered in this world created in accordance with a holy intention.
     May God's intentions be fulfilled
          in our lives, during our days,
          in the time of this abiding,
          quickly, yea soon,
and let us say, Amen.

The Holy One, blessed be God, forgives and rejoices.   Amen.

Blessed and praised, sung about and told in tales,
     honored and made widely known,
     be the name of the Holy One, blessed be God.
The mercy of God exceeds praises.
The loving justice of God overshadows all blessings that we can express.
     (God is more than all songs, more than all stories.
     God is more than all that can be spoken by human voices.)
     And let us say, Amen.

Tell of the Lord who forgives and rejoices.   Amen.

Unto your house, unto all tellers of tales, unto all listeners and those who hear, and unto those who listen and who retell the tales, unto all who embrace the study of God's story, in this place or in any other place, unto them and unto you be understanding,

be mercy,
be the sacrifice of your hearts,
be forgiveness,
be redeeming love,
be recovery from sin,
be fruitfulness,
be rejoicing from our God who is in heaven,
and let us say, Amen.

Hallowed be the name of the God.   Amen.

Create in me a clean heart, O God.   Amen.

May there be peace for us from heaven.
May we be forgiven.
May we rejoice,
and let us say, Amen.

O Lord, open thou my lips and my mouth shall show forth thy praise.   Amen.

May our God who makes peace in heaven
make peace for us on earth,
and let us say, Amen.

Passage

YHWH, I come.

YHWH, many are we here,
	walking this Jerusalem road.
Many are we who have come to love him.
We journey together like the gathered exiles
	summoned by God's shofar.
Most of us Jews, of course, for he is a Jew,
	observing the kindly Law,
	teaching from our ancient scripture,
	healing in the Spirit of the living God.

There are others from various places
	who have come to be here, too.

Like Ruth they come from distant persuasions,
	finding in our living God
	and in our Rebbe
	a loving truth they long for.
Like Ruth they come, persuaded by love
	to cast their lot with us.
Like Ruth many become one with us in deed
	and journey by our side.

Ruth is among my son's progenitors,
	a woman called like Abraham and Sarah
	from her land of origin into a strange place.

Like us she beat a path upon a road of God's design,
	listening to love, she heard and answered;
	choosing the better part, she came;
	thirsting, she drank at YHWH's well.

Ruth, Woman Redeemer of Naomi

Her Story...

The Book of Ruth

It happened in the days when judges judged
    that there was a famine in the land.
Naomi, Elimelech and their two sons
    went out from Bethlechem-judah
    to sojourn in the field of Moab.
    There they settled and
    Elimelech died.
Naomi and her two sons continued in Moab, the sons
    both joining Moab women to wife,
    Ruth and Orpha now daughters in Naomi's home.
And it happened after ten years
    that Naomi's two sons died,
        leaving her without sons and husband.

Naomi rose up to return
    from her sojourn in the field of Moab,
    having heard that YHWH had visited her people
    and there was bread again in the land.
With her daughters-in-law
    she took the road of return to the land of Judah.

At the border she turned to her daughters, saying:

39

Go. Turn back, my daughters.
    Return you to your mother's house.
    Go. Turn back, my daughters,
        I have nothing with which to care for us.

Weeping, one turned back to her mother's house,
    having fulfilled her duty.
Weeping, one continued on.

The one who continued was Ruth.

    Do not press me to turn round from you.
    Do not beg me to return.

    Wherever you journey, I will journey,
        I will lodge where you lodge.

    I will drink of the well of life as you drink,
        being still when you are still.

    Your way I will make my way;
        in ritual observance will I delight.

    Your God will be my God,
        beloved in the passion of my heart.

    When you return to dust, I will accompany you;
        in the house of your ancestors
        I will live with you forever.

    May God deal justly with me and more so
        if anything but death keep me from this vow.

With these words Ruth showed herself as she truly was,

a woman living all that Israel at its best would strive to be,
a woman of integrity, deeply and profoundly kind.
Our foremother showing forth God's image in covenantal kindness,
coming to Judah out of the field of Moab.

Naomi knew of a man named Boaz,
her kin by covenant.
Ruth, a stranger, went to work
harvesting the corner of the fields,
gleaning in the sheaves as was her right.
And it happened that the fields belonged to Boaz.

According to the ways of Israel, prescribed by their caring God,
the right to work the corner of the field, following the harvesters,
was given to the stranger, the widow, the poor, and the levite
so that they might work with honest effort,
so that they never need know
the shame of begging from another.

Boaz watched her labor,
for word of her kindness had come to him
from all sides.

Have you not heard, my daughter,
you are not to go to another field,
neither leave this one?
Abide here with the women who harvest.
You will be cared for.
You will be given from the well.

She knelt, bending humbly,

How have I found favor in your eyes?
You have considered me when I am a stranger!

Boaz responded,

> Word of your kindness comes from all sides.
> May the Lord God of Israel do to you as you have done to Naomi.
> May thy wage of kindness be full and complete
>> from the Lord God under the shadow of whose wings
>> you have sought refuge.

And Ruth continued,

> May I always find favor in your eyes,
>> for you have comforted me.
> You have spoken to the heart of your handmaid
>> though you do not know me.

Then Boaz offered her bread and wine.

At the end of the day Ruth returned to the city
> with food from her work,
>> which she brought out and gave to Naomi.
Naomi prayed her thanksgiving,

> May the one who acknowledged you be blessed!

Ruth told Naomi the name of the man
> with whom she had worked,
>> the name of Boaz.

> Again Naomi prayed,

> Blessed be God who has not forgotten kindness
>> neither with the living nor with the dead.

The man is our kin by covenant,

one of those commissioned
to redeem those like ourselves.
Go, glean as you have told me
with the women of the harvest.
Ruth worked through the weeks of the barley harvest
and through the weeks of the wheat harvest;
afterward she remained at home with Naomi,
dwelling there.
And it happened then that Naomi said to her,

My daughter, my peace is in your security.
Tonight Boaz winnows barley
on the threshing floor near the gate.
Boaz is among our covenant-kin
who have assumed the responsibility of redemption.

Naomi instructed Ruth in the cultic ways of Israel,
whereby some were responsible
for the security of others.
Ruth washed herself, anointed herself, put on her mantle
and went walking through the city to the city gate
out to the threshing floor. Here she waited.
When Boaz had worked, eaten and drunk,
and his heart was merry,
he did lay down.

Ruth did everything as Naomi had commanded her.

Early in the night she came softly,
uncovered him and lay herself down.
In the midst of the night,
he awoke shaken, and found her.

Who are you?

I am Ruth, your handmaid.
Overshadow your handmaid with your wing.

Blessed may you be by the Lord our God, my daughter.
You have again shown kindness to us in your wisdom.
You have chosen the ways of respect and honor
    within the gates of our people.
        You are virtuous. You are worthy.

When the night was past,
    Boaz cared for Ruth the stranger and Naomi her mother,
    securing for them the redeeming mercy of the people of Israel.
The deeds were drawn.
The witnesses at the gate proclaiming,

We are witnesses this day.
May the Lord God bless you.
Like Rachel and like Leah,
    who between them built the house of Israel,
    may you be fruitful in this land.
May you be a matriarch in Bethlechem-judah.
May your house become as the house of Perez, your forebearer,
    whom the young Tamar bore to the Patriarch Judah,
    secured from the seed which God shall give you.

And it happened in this way that Boaz took Ruth to him,
    she became his wife;
    he came to her and went into her.
The Lord God made her to conceive and
    she bore a son.
The women said to Naomi,

Blessed be YHWH, who this day has provided for you a near-kin.
May the child's name be called out in Israel.
He will be life to you and

sustenance in your later years.
By the graciousness of YHWH
Ruth, the daughter who loves you, has borne him to you.
She is more to you than seven sons.

Naomi clasped the child to her breast and became nurse to him.
The neighboring women rejoiced calling aloud,

A son is born to Naomi!
Calling his name to be Obed,
the women named him,
and he was the father of Jesse,
who was the father of David.

Now this is the lineage of Obed and Jesse and of David,
which began with Perez,
whose mother was Tamar,
who redeemed her heritage from Judah of Israel.

Kaddish of Remembering

YHWH, in the telling of Ruth's story
I see your will for us more clearly.
Hearken to my Kaddish of remembering.
Teach me, my God.
In the lives of those who image you
I come to know you as you really are.

Abundant and gracious is God's name
in all the earth,
the earth shaped by God's design.
May God's will be done

in our lives, during our days,
in the time of our times,
soon, speedily, even this day,
and let us say, Amen.

God's people will be my people.   Amen.

Beloved and praised,
respected in the annals of all people on earth,
remembered in our whisperings,
blessed be the name of God
(though God be more than all our tellings)
and let us say, Amen.

Your handmaid desires to find favor in your eyes.   Amen.

Unto these your people, unto all rabbis, masters and witnesses, unto all
their disciples, unto all who seek for the telling of the deeds of YHWH in
this house or in any other house, unto them and to you
be wisdom,
be vows of fidelity,
be the kindness of redeemers,
be a fruitful life and
generous gifts from our God who is in heaven,
and let us say, Amen.

YHWH, in the shadow of your wings I will take shelter.   Amen.

May our houses be built up in YHWH.
The fruit of our bearing be joy for others
and sustenance in their later years,

and let us say, Amen.

You are my covenant redeemer.   Amen.

May God's peace in heaven
     be our peace on earth,
     and let us say, Amen.

Passage

YHWH, I come.

YHWH, many are we here,
     walking this Jerusalem road.

Many are we who have come to love him.
We journey together like the gathered exiles,
     summoned by God's shofar.

These are the days of Pesach.
The road crowded with pilgrims
     over-spills the trail,
          pouring its colorful collective
               onto the sideways.

Non-Jews stare in passing,
     call us exclusive, different.
Non-Jews step away in passing,
     shy from our intensity.

Jews settle in the days of observance,
    customary foods, ritual and melody.
The feast takes on the mantle
    of these days and time.
We feast on freedom,
    defined in God's tongue,
    remembering our redeeming,
    remembering our passover.

There were hoshanas and procession
    last week when he joined us here,
    looking for all the world
    like Solomon on David's mule
    being led by Bathsheba and Nathan
    to the Lord's anointing.
Today the mood has changed
    and we are deep into the grappling,
    our minds and spirits eye to eye
    with what it means to be God's own.
I gather myself for the time ahead.
    Walking,
        I must return to my remembering.
Gathering myself for the time ahead, I recall again his heritage.
The strength and faith of those who have gone before us will
    be sorely needed in the coming hours.

YHWH, as the moment nears, come close,
    I must clear my mind with remembering.

His foremother, Rahab.
    What life!
    What a legacy of spirited courage!
She the first in our ancient scriptural litany of ancestors
    to reside outside the cult of Israel
        yet comprehend

the full domain of YHWH.
Others had declared YHWH was God.
    Others even, God alone.
Rahab proclaimed YHWH
    God of Olam.
    Olam . . . heaven and earth,
        all creation perceived and unperceived,
        past, present, yet to come,
        forever and forever and forever.

Rahab is among my son's progenitors,
    a woman called to cast her life
    at the feet of YHWH.

Like Rahab,
    many have come,
    believing what they hear.
Like Rahab,
    they have acted on their belief.
Like Rahab,
    covenantal promises have been made and kept.

Rahab, the innkeeper,
    the harlot, some say.
Like us she acted on her belief,
    casting her lot with Judah's tribe,
    gathering many under her wing,
    securing her redeeming passover.
Rahab survived and lived
    to build a house of prophets in Israel.

Rahab, Woman Who Heard, Believed and Accomplished

Her Story . . . *Joshua 2;6:1-25*

Rahab kept an inn by the gates,
    close within the double wall of Jericho,
    a public house set within the mix of things,
    fraught with comings and goings.
Some called it a brothel.
Some called Rahab a harlot.

From Joshua two young spying men came to Jericho,
    to the house of Rahab.

    (God had opened her door and she welcomed them.)

They came and lodged there.

It was reported to the ruler of Jericho
    that men had come to Rahab's house
    that very night from the children of Israel.

Soldiers stood outside her door. They shouted, but entered not:

Bring out the men who entered your house this very night
   for they are spies.

Rahab led Joshua's men to the roof,
   hiding them amongst the stalks of flax she had been drying.
   She returned to answer the authorities.

   (God opened her mouth and she spoke with cleverness.)

She connived to set the authorities on a fruitless search,
   and they went rushing to follow her deceptive directions.

Rahab approached the men of Joshua
   whom she had concealed amongst the flax stalks,
   speaking most earnestly,

   I know
      that YHWH your God
         has promised you this land.

   (God had opened her ears and she had listened and heard.)

   I know
      that YHWH your God is a holy warrior
      who achieves victory,
         not with violent weapons held in your hands.

   I know
      YHWH is the holy warrior
         who accompanies you,
            casting fear like a shadow to wither the will of your foes.

   Jericho's rulers grow faint and melt in their hearts.

   (God had opened her eyes and she perceived the terror-stricken.)

I know
    YHWH your God dried up the water of the Sea of Reeds
        that you might cross safely when you came out of Egypt.
I know also what happened to other rulers who stood in your way.

(God had opened her mind and she believed.)

I know when we heard these things,
        our hearts melted.
When we spoke of these
        our spirits ran out of us like water.

(God opened her soul and she proclaimed.)

I know your God YHWH is indeed God.
God of the heavens above.
God of the earth beneath.

(God opened her heart and she covenanted with them.)

Swear to me now by YHWH your God
    who is God indeed.
Show mercy as I have shown you mercy.
As I have been kind,
        extend the kindness of your covenant
            to me and to my house.

Give me a sign—a token of trust between us—
        that all of my house shall be saved,
        my mother and father, my brothers and sisters,
        all who gather under my roof in my care.
        Deliver our lives from death.

And the men answered her, vowing,

Our life for yours and the lives of your families.
If a treaty of silence remains with you
    we will honor you with safety
    when we come into the land
    the Lord gives us.
Trust and good faith will be between us.

  (God opened her spirit and she trusted them, resting in their promise.)

In the sleeping city, in the silence of the dead of night,
Rahab lowered Joshua's men from a window by means of a bundled
    cord,
    for her house was within the double walls by the gate of Jericho
    and she dwelt there in the structure of the fortress.

She whispered to them,

    Get you into the hills for safety where those who search for you
    will not find you. Hide yourselves three days and after that return
    your own way.
They gave her a scarlet cord to tie at her window
    from which she had worked their escape,
    a sign of their covenant to return her kindness.
They gave her a blood red band to mark her lintel post
    and be passed over in the dying.

In this manner she became as one with Israel.

They promised,

    Whoever is fast within your house shall be yours to redeem.
    Responsibility for your chosen people will be on our heads;
        no hand will be laid upon them.

Rahab responded,

There is trust and loyalty between us.
Whatever we have agreed, according to your word,
    so shall it be.

The men who had come into Jericho to spy did as Rahab had advised
them. They cast their steps to the hills.

When they returned to Joshua they reported all that had happened,
    giving Joshua Rahab's intelligence.

    Truly, she tells us,
    the Lord has given into our hands the whole land,
    for even the people lose courage
    when they hear of what YHWH does for us.

Rahab was their only informant.
    They relied totally on her intelligence.
        She was all they had need of.
    She spoke truly and
        God had opened their ears to her.

And it happened as Rahab had told them.

The children of Israel rose early on the seventh day,
    encircling the town as they had done each of the six earlier days,
    shutting up the people within the city with fear,
    encircling the city, processing silently in all their cultic splendor.

At the seventh circle round the city on that seventh day
    the priests lifted their trumpets and blew forth a mighty sound.
    Joshua said to the Israelites,

    Lift your voices. Shout!
        The Lord has given us Jericho.

All therein save the house of Rahab will be brought down.
Rahab, the keeper of the inn, and
    all who have sought sanctuary with her are to live
        because she believed the word of YHWH.
Concealing our messengers she has redeemed her people.
Keep your covenant with her.

And so the two men who had been concealed by Rahab's kindness
    went in to her house and brought out safely all who belonged to her,
    and they were settled beside the Israelites' encampment.
Though the city was destroyed,
    Rahab, the house of Rahab,
        and all within the house of Rahab were saved alive.

Rahab became of the faithful of Israel's God.

    (God opened her womb and she bore sons and daughters who became
        prophets of YHWH.)

Rahab dwells in Israel to this day.

Kaddish of Remembering

YHWH, remembering Rahab and her redeeming faith
    calls back to my mind your purposes for us.
You desire all of us to recognize you as you are.
    YHWH, the holy warrior,
        you accompany those who speak your name.
        You mark the threshhold of their lives
            so that violence may pass over them.
YHWH, holy warrior, mark us all.

Redeem us in the coming violence according to your will for us.
YHWH, your way is a mystery of loving kindness.
I trust you.
Whatever the way, I will walk it.
Hear my Kaddish of remembering.

Mighty and trustworthy is the name of God
in all the world, within all life which God created,
according to a holy will.
May God's will be done
on earth as in heaven,
in your lifetime, during your days,
during the span of the people Israel,
soon, with haste,
and let us say, Amen.

The Holy One, blessed be God, redeems those who show
kindness.   Amen.

Blessed, revered and hallowed,
lifted up in memory and made familiar among peoples,
beloved be the name of God
(though God be beyond all tellings, more than all the words we can
express)
and let us say, Amen.

God opens our hearts and we proclaim the greatness of
YHWH.   Amen.

Be faithful with acts as well as with words.   Amen.

Unto those here listening, unto those who remember and impart the story, unto all teachers who teach, unto all who teach again what they have been taught, unto all who immerse themselves in the learning of scriptures—unto all these

> be courage,
> be mercy as mercy is shown by you,
> be nourishment for the mind,
> be rescue,
> be faithful fulfillment of vows,
> be words to accompany deeds,
> be understanding of the true nature of God,
> be peace from our God who is in heaven,
>> and let us say, Amen.

Our God YHWH is God of heaven and earth, beginnings and endings,
> all things understood and not understood, forever and
> forever.   Amen.

May we cast our lot with the people of God.
May we redeem all people in our care with our convictions.
May we join the camp of YHWH.
And say you, Amen.

Praise YHWH, the holy warrior who accompanies the believer in
peace.   Amen.

Passage

YHWH, I come.

YHWH, many are we here,

walking this Jerusalem road.
Many are we who have come to love him.
    We journey together like the gathered exiles
    summoned by God's shofar.

The road begins to twist and turn as we come nearer.
    The stones are slippery beneath my feet.
Harder and harder the travel.
Obedience to this way of ours has been my life's delight,
    save for today
        when I seem to carry the sighs of all our people,
            burdening within my breast.
Obedience to this way of ours changes, of course,
    with each of us who lives it,
    grows in spirit with each one of us who carries it along.
Obedience to this way of ours
    has been our gift to one another,
    drawing us within the saving scope of God.

I must center in remembering, lest I falter,
    holding my mind anchored,
    securing my soul in who I am.
Walking, I return to a beginning time,
    the ancient ones whose deeds ferment our own.
    Tamar, the believer, giant of spirit,
        weaving her steady way through our history.

Like Tamar we would stand tall,
    trusting in the truth of YHWH's law.
Like Tamar we would stand steadfast,
    pursuing purity of purpose all the while.
Like Tamar we would bring the clarity of vision
    to those who still deny our calling,
        who still think themselves the only righteous,
        who quiver, bending to the shadow of Rome.

Tamar is among my son's progenitors,
    a woman who trusted in God's way.
Like us, spending her life in rigorous pursuit of righteousness,
    creating bold plans to live her dream,
    returning Judah to the promise of his heritage.

Tamar triumphed over shame,
    establishing a house of peace and prophecy in Israel.

TAMAR, WOMAN WHO TRUSTED IN THE LORD'S WAY

Her Story... *Genesis 38*

Tamar was named for the Tamar tree.
    Tamar the remarkable,
      Tamar the good.
    Her story is told in our tents today,
      and many the daughters named with her name.

Judah was born the fourth son of Jacob and Leah,
    brothering the young Joseph,
    pleading his life as he lay in the pit.
    Judah was righteous.

Judah became the brother of Dinah,
    leading his clan on an angry spree,
    avenging the rape of Dinah.
    Judah was righteous.

Judah wived outside the cult
    to Shuah, daughter of Canaan.
    Three sons were born to them.

And it happened when the time came
        that Judah secured for his first-born
        a daughter of Israel for him to wife.
        Her name was Tamar.

Tamar named for the Tamar tree.
        Tamar the stately,
            Tamar the tall.
        Tamar the daughter of a priestly family,
            faithful, observant Jew.

She came to the clan of Judah
        expecting to increase the house of Israel.
Judah's Canaanite sons had other thoughts.
Her husband,
        Er his name,
        was raucus in the sight of God.
        Ungodly ways were his undoing
            and he died.

Tamar named for the Tamar tree.
        Tamar the modest,
            Tamar the pure.

Tamar received from Judah
        his second son, Onan,
        as was the leverite law.
        Tamar's sacred task to build up the
            house of YHWH in Israel.
Again, the folly of unruly sons.
        Onan, jealous of his brother and bitter,
        humiliated and deceived her.
        He also brought himself down with ungodliness
            and died.

Tamar named for the Tamar tree.
    Tamar the thoughtful,
      Tamar the strong.

The legends tell of the woman Tamar,
    stately and beautiful,
    gentle and faithful,
    persistent in the ways of Israel.

Twice left by ungodly men,
    the wife secured by Judah for his sons
    sought her legal inheritance from him.
    Judah, the righteous, put her off.

He did not do the honorable thing,
    releasing her with her name and property,
    but promised her a third husband from his rowdy clan,
    a son yet too young to wed.

    Return you to your family home, he said,
    when he is of age I will
    restore you to my house.

She returned to her village and dwelt there,
    thoughtfully,
    attendant to her heritage,
      observant daughter of Israel.

Tamar named for the Tamar tree.
    Tamar the steadfast,
      Tamar the wise.

The days multiplied
    after the time of the promised son had passed,

after the time of Tamar's mother-in-law's dying,
after the time of Judah's consoling.

Judah came up for the festival of shearing and
    Tamar set out with plans to
        waylay him at the crossroads.

Tamar named for the Tamar tree.
    Tamar the certain,
        Tamar the firm.

Tamar changed her mantle of widowhood,
    covering her face with a veil and
    waited.

Judah, up for the shearing,
    approached her.

And she took him . . . with wisdom,
    she took his seal,
    she took his cord,
    she took his staff,
    she took his seed.

Tamar secured her inheritance.

Tamar named for the Tamar tree.
    Tamar the merciful,
        Tamar the just.

She turned back on the road,
    resumed her mantle of widowhood,
    returned home and waited.

Judah sent servants to reclaim his goods.

None in the village had seen a harlot there at the crossroads.
None such as these had ever been there, they said.

Tamar named for the Tamar tree.
    Tamar the upright,
       Tamar the merciful.

Tamar watched and waited.
Three months passed.
Tamar grew thick.
Gossips hustled the word to Judah
    who raged . . .

    Burn her!
      (A brand or death,
         the tale is unclear.
         For a levite daughter
         the price was heavy.)

    Burn her!
      he strutted in righteous ranting.
    Bring her forward and punish her here!

And she came quietly and with integrity,
    never condemning him publicly.

Tamar named for the Tamar tree.
    Tamar the decent,
       Tamar the bold.

She came privately,
    sending word before her to Judah.

    It is by the man whose goods these are
      that I am with child.

In truth, Judah discern for yourself
    the owner
    of this seal, this cord, this staff.

Judah recognized them and
    acknowledged his own.

He stood openly before the people,
    naked of heart,
    confessing,

    She is more righteous than I.

And he respected her thereafter.

Tamar bore twin sons and
    raised them up with honor.
Israel remembers them as mighty men,
    sons of Judah who regained
    his righteousness in her.
Her heritage thrives in a line of judges, kings and prophets,
    righteous all as she was righteous.

Tamar named for the Tamar tree.
    Tamar the matriarch,
        Tamar the great.

Kaddish of Remembering

YHWH, in merciful obedience is your heritage sustained.
    Grant me the fullness of faithful love
        according to the people in whom I was born.

My God, I would stand tall as Tamar stood
        in these coming hours.
        In the face of violent death
        may my mind and my heart
        be for justice and mercy.
May we yet raise up for you a house of honor in Israel.
Hearken to my Kaddish of remembering
        and teach me, O my Master.

Great and holy be the name of God,
        praised in all the world,
        which was created by God's will.
May God reclaim this holy inheritance
        in our lives, in our days,
        in our households,
        quickly, even at a near time,
        and let us say, Amen.

Blessed be the inheritance of God.   Amen.

Sought after and honored be the name of God
        (though God be beyond all imaginings,
            more steadfast than all our faithfulness)
        and let us say, Amen.

Let all those who seek justice secure it.   Amen.

Let all those who hold the name of another in their hands be
merciful.   Amen.

Unto all you listeners, unto all storytellers, unto all you who retell the
stories generation after generation, all you who delight in the learning of

Holy Scripture here in this place or in any other place, unto you and to them
      be laughter and singing,
      be new meanings from scripture,
      be long life in the treasure of your traditions,
      be friendship and strong spirits,
      be faithfulness to your heritage
      and redeeming kindness from our God
         who is in heaven,
      and let us say, Amen.

In the Lord's way do I put my trust.   Amen.

May we establish the heritage of God in our land,
      in our time,
      and may our claiming bring wisdom and honor, prophecy and
         peace
      to all lands, in all times,
      and let us say, Amen.

May we establish a house of honor in Israel.   Amen.

May our loving God who hears the praises of angels in heaven
      hear our praises on earth
      and rejoice in peace,
      and let us say, Amen.

The Journey Continued

YHWH, I come.

YHWH, we walk the road,
    this last mile,
      so close together.
Those who love him
    walking,
      a huddled company.

Whatever happens next
    we will continue,
      sojourners in your house
      as we have always been.

YHWH, we draw near to this last place
    believing,
      trusting in the promise you have been.

YHWH, whatever happens next we will continue faithful,
    observing Torah,
      imaging you.

God, blessed be the Holy One,
    never asks of us that which
    God, the Holy One,
    has not first performed.
God teaches by example;
    we learn by looking on these samplings;
    we live by learning.
God walks where we walk.
How often have you, YHWH, stood where I will soon stand?
How many times have you been where I will be?
Each of us in this steadfast company come willingly here,
    walking your pathway,
    praying as we come,
    hallowing this ground, this time, these lives,

forgiving as the violence is done,
believing as we stand our holy watch with him
    that in this simple act of kindness
    earth is made more kind.

PART TWO: LEARNING

God asks us to
> image with our lives the God we see.
God requires us to sanctify the earth
> with Godly doings.
God gifts us with security and holy company.

YHWH, whatever happens next I will continue faithful;
> believing in your love, I carry on.
> I will remain here standing steadfast.
> God, my only God, come stand with me.

YHWH, I remain here anchored in remembering,
> knowing that tomorrow's time will come.
> I will not die here standing steadfast.
> Adonai, lord of my heart, come live with me.

YHWH, tomorrow and tomorrow I will be here,
> living Torah taught us by my son.
I will live and spread the teaching.
Not one word of his life will be lost.
We are a people of remembering, no life is lost.
> We will sustain you,
> telling the stories,
> recalling the moments,
> passing on the yearning image we have been.

YHWH, I live these hours in silence,
> deepened in the stillness of our hearts,
> etched in the hours, sounds of anguish,
> chiseled forever in the stories of this time.
These are not the only sounds that we will echo.
> Never, never will we let the story die.
> Words strong on the hillside,
>   emblazoned on our memory,
>   will not die. They live forever.

Strong Torah taught with loving is the life he called us to.
> Never, never will we let the learning die.

KADDISH OF THE BEATITUDES

Matthew 5:3-11

Abundant and precious is the name of God
    here in this earth
    created so lovingly by the word of the Creative One.

May God's creation be made holy
    in our lifetime, during our days,
    within the events of this age,
    now, even now,
    and let us say, Amen.

We come to the learning, O Lord. Teach us your ways.   Amen.

If you are humble of spirit
    you will be welcomed in God's household.   Amen.

If you mourn over your shortfallings
    you will be held in God's comfort.   Amen.

If you trust in the power of kindness
    you will inherit the caring of God's earth.   Amen.

If you seek justice and mercy for others,
    thirsting after it, yes even hungering,
    you will be nourished on the food of God.   Amen.

If you are merciful
     you will receive mercy.   Amen.

    If you have clean hands,
    if you have a broken heart,
    if you keep a constant mind
      directed toward living God's careful way,
    you will see God.   Amen.

If you are a maker of peace
    you will be God's family.   Amen.

When you are the object of contempt for your obedience,
     when you suffer to follow this way,
    you will find yourselves
      blessed . . . awakened in God . . .
    because you have been faithful,
    and let us say, Amen.

With these teachings, O Lord, may we make your earth holy.   Amen.

May our living the graceful life in this world
    bring honor and love to the
    name of God . . . blessed be shalom
    (though God is more peace than all our understanding
      lived in this world)
    and let us say, Amen.

Unto all of you here with us, unto all rabbis, unto all disciples,
unto all disciples of disciples, and unto all who entrust themselves
to the holy study of Torah in this place, or in any other place,
unto them all and unto you
      be humbleness of spirit,
      be mourning of your shortfallings,
      be trust in the power of kindness,
      be hunger and thirst in the pursuit of justice and mercy for others,
      be mercifulness,
      be cleanness, contrition and constancy,
      be peacemaking,
      be faithfulness in the presence of those who reject you,
      be blessedness in the company of our God,
      and say you, Amen.

With these teachings may we hallow God's name.   Amen.

My help is in God.   Amen.

May our God who desires peace for all people
      accompany us in the making of peace on earth,
      and let us say, Amen.

KADDISH OF THE LAW

Matthew 5:17-20

Magnify the Lord with me.
>By the word of God the earth was made.
>God spoke and it was created.
>God commanded and there it stood.

May God's word be fulfilled on earth,
>during our days, during our life,
>during our times,
>yea soon, yea soon,
>and let us say, Amen.

We come to the learning, O Lord. Teach us your ways.

You have heard it said that there was one who came to set aside the Law,
>and I say to you that one came
>to set the Law more deeply in your hearts.   Amen.

I say to you, you are each called
>to extend the meaning of the Law.   Amen.

I say to you, you are created for
>continuing in the Law,
>dwelling in God,
>rooting yourselves in shalom.   Amen.

Truly, truly you are called to abiding obedience
        to the Law in its eternal fullness.
        No part of it shall pass away until there is peace.
Truly, truly I say to you,
        be Torah-true . . . intensify your living.
        Love is the fulfillment of the Law.
        Search out God's heart within each word,
            fill it full with your loving
            and carry on from there.   Amen.

I say to you, live and teach the loving Law
        and you will be considered precious in God's place.   Amen.

You have heard it said that religious leaders exemplify the Law.
        I say to you, each one of you is responsible for the Law.
        I say to you, let your love of God and of neighbor
                exceed even these good teachers
        so that God's household may be put aright.   Amen.

With these teachings, O Lord, may we make your earth holy.   Amen.

May our living a life of blessedness,
        abiding obediently in the living law,
        bringing knowledge of the living God
            who abides faithfully with us,
            seed love into every corner of the world
        (though God's abiding faithfulness,
            God's adherence to the kindly law
            surpasses all human obedience)
        and let us say, Amen.

Unto us all, unto all who clarify the Law, unto all who live and teach
the Law, and to those who follow after their living and their teaching
here in this place, and in every place, unto all them and to you
      be devotedness,
      be abiding obedience,
      be love intensified,
      be abundant striving,
      be Torah truth,
      be upholding of God's word,
      be teachings and learnings,
      be sweet living.
May God grant that you will be fulfillment of the holy loving Law,
      and you will be considered precious
      in God's place,
      and let us say, Amen.

Come, fulfill the Law with me.   Amen.

Dwell in love and carry on.   Amen.

May the word of YHWH which is integrity itself
      dwell with you as peace for God's world,
      and let us say, Amen.

KADDISH OF THE LIFE-SPIRIT

Matthew 5:21-24

Great and holy be the name of God
    on this earth,
    built in God's wisdom.
    May God's wisdom prevail on the earth
    during our days, within our lives,
    in the workings of our nations,
    right soon, even quickly,
    and let us say, Amen.

We come to the learning, O Lord. Teach us your ways.   Amen.

You have heard it said,
    You shall not murder.
    Those who kill people deserve the unholy name
        "shedders of blood."
And I say to you,
    Each person on earth is God's image.
    Shed not the blood of the image of God.   Amen.

You have heard it said,
    It is YHWH alone who gives life and
    it is YHWH alone who gives death.

And I say to you,
    What YHWH bestows
    YHWH will watch over
    Let no one take away life.   Amen.

You have heard it said,
    To berate others
        so that their cheeks turn pale and
            their pulsing stops
     is like the shedding of blood;
     from their faces and from their hearts which image God
        has the blood been drained.

And I say to you, anyone who heaps anger on another
    shall be liable in the community.   Amen.

You have heard it said,
    To shame others
        so that their cheeks flush red
         and their pulsing increases
    is like the inner shedding of blood.

And I say to you, anyone who shames another
    shall be accountable among us.   Amen.

You have heard it said,
    To gossip, to insult, to dishonor or ridicule
           is to undermine a reputation,
           is like unto the shedding of blood.
    A good name is like the lifting up of God's name.
And I say to you, if you say such things of your neighbor
    you shall answer for it in God's presence.   Amen.

You have heard it said,
    You are the children of God,
    the builders of God's household.
    Only so long as you build up God's name in one another
    shall you be builders.
And I say to you,
    Whoever calls another "fool" or "disobedient of God"
    shall be in danger of falling away altogether. Amen.

Therefore, if you bring your gifts to the altar and
    remember as you approach
    that you are not reconciled with another,
    leave your gift beside the altar,
    go quickly, make peace with that one.
    Reconciled, come again to the altar,
    lift up the gift of your offering and offer it,
    and let us say, Amen.

With these teachings, O Lord, may we make your earth holy.   Amen.

Protect, preserve and hold precious the image of God in this
earth.   Amen.

May our gentle cherishing of the life-spirit
    bring holy wonder to the name of God
    (though God cherishes life beyond all our imagining)
    and let us say, Amen.

Unto this house and this nation, unto all people within,
unto all prophets and teachers of the peaceful way, unto their witnesses

and disciples and those who follow them, in this place, and in all places,
unto them and unto you
     be thoughtful speaking,
     be gentle ways,
     be cherishing of life,
     be fruitfulness,
     be abundance of disciples
        to listen and perform peaceful acts,
     be companionship,
     be simple pleasures and deep joy,
     be deeds of loving kindness,
     be all things put right
         in the presence of our loving God
         whose heaven is a peaceful earth,
         and let us say, Amen.

Go out reconciling yourselves with one another.   Amen.

Let us spend ourselves lifting up the lives of others.   Amen.

May our God whose name is shalom
     hearken to our work for reconciling peace and
     abide with us,
     and let us say, Amen.

KADDISH OF MORAL ACTS

Matthew 5:27-40

Supreme and sacred be the name of God
    in the world fashioned according to God's will.
May God's will be done on earth as in heaven,
    this day, our day, in our history,
    and let us say, Amen.

We come to the learning, O Lord. Teach us your ways.   Amen.

The body is the temple of God;
    the soul within proclaims God's name.
Five doorways to the world of the soul has God created.
Doorways through which God comes and goes.

At each doorway is posted a watch:
    the watchers' names,
        vision . . . hearing . . . smell . . . taste . . . touch.
The Lord said to Moses,
    Who is it who makes your mouth,
      your speech and your hearing?
    Is it not I, the Lord!
    I will be with thee and teach thee.   Amen.

You have heard it said,
    Do not lure the faithful from their authenticity.
    Do not rob God of God's own.
    Do not endanger the fidelity of mind,
        of heart or of body to God's Law.
    Who so robbeth the Father in heaven or the Mother on earth
        the same is the companion of the destroyer.
And I say to you,
    The eye that lusts and the hand that lures
        are better cast away.
    That which causes you to stumble is useless.   Amen.

You have heard it said,
    Marriage can be severed with a legal deed alone.
And I say to you,
    Marriages vowed in the presence of God
        are governed by God,
        bound and loosed according to the wisdom of God.
    Let none of you in your legalities,
        in your gossip or in your hand of neighboring,
        impair the judgment and mercy of God
        between husband and wife.   Amen.

You have heard it said,
    Be true to your words.
    Take not the name of the Lord in vain.
And I say to you also,
    Embellish not your pledging.
    Say simply what you intend.

    Let your "Yes" be fulfilled.
    Let your "No" stand firm.   Amen.

You have heard it said, Take no more in injury
    than has been done to you.
And I tell you, extend yourself.
    When injury is done to you
    respond with love,
    and let us say, Amen.

With these teachings, O Lord, may we make your earth holy.   Amen.

Blessed, praised and glorified be the name of God.
May our living and doing praise God and our actions leaven heavy
        hearts.
    May our lives' light shine
        to the gain of this world
    (though God's light shining in each human heart
        is beyond our understanding)
    and let us say, Amen.

By our hearing and doing may we praise God.   Amen.

Unto all rabbis and teachers who struggle to teach moral acts, unto all
rabbis and teachers who struggle to live what they teach, unto all
learners who teach with the model of their lives, unto all people now and
to come who seek to be images of God on this earth, unto all of these and
unto you here this day
    be holy speech and vision,
    be fidelity,
    be cherishing of another's fidelity,
    be compassionate judging,
    be frequent mercy,
    be clear words and firm resolve,
    be the integrity of repaying those you have hurt
        according to the measure you have done in injury,

be cooperation in disputes,
be loving responses,
be joy in this peaceful way,
   and let us say, Amen

May God shine in our lives for the good of this earth.   Amen.

May our God who desires us to live
      with justice and mercy
      in equal measures
      make plain the path before our feet,
      and let us say, Amen.

Let us incline our ear to God's ways,
      our eyes to the best in each other,
      our hearts to God's peace,
      and let us say, Amen.

 KADDISH OF NEIGHBORS

Matthew 5:43-48

Hallowed be God's name,
    hallowed in this world which the Holy One
    made to perfection.
May God perfect this world
    in our lives, in our days, in our times,
    soon, yes soon,
    and let us say, Amen.

We come to the learning, O Lord. Teach us your ways.   Amen.

You have heard it said,
    Love your neighbors.

And I say to you, extend love to all people,
    even your enemies,
    for all are God's children.   Amen.

Remember your neighbors in Egypt . . .
    the friends of your heart
      whom you loved with a love
      like that of God resting upon the tabernacle.

Remember these your "sh'chein chem"
    who assisted you in your escape from Egypt,
      giving generously of their possessions,
      adorning your sons and daughters with their treasure.

Remember your neighbors whom God called "sh'chein chem,"
    how you gathered them into your homes
    to eat the lamb of protection with you,
    how you gathered them in behind the blood-marked doors.
Remember these Egyptians who were neighbors,
    whom you loved with a love like that of God
            resting upon the tabernacle.
            "Sh'chein chem" are to be found wherever
            people reach out to one another in love,
            and let us say, Amen.

Remember at the Sea of Reeds,
    God's intent that the children of Israel escape
            without bloodshed;
    only the Egyptians rushed in pursuit, falling there.
Neither rejoice nor gloat over their suffering.
Grieve as your God grieves,
            for the Egyptians are children of God.   Amen.

I call to mind with you:
    God causes rain to fall on all fields
            and the sun to shine on all households.
Be like your God,
    cause your goodness to rain on all places,
            the light of your kindness on all households,
    for you are created in the holy image.
Your God is gracious and merciful without end.
Be as enduringly gracious
    and merciful as God is,
    and let us say, Amen.

With these teachings, O Lord, may we make your earth holy.   Amen.

Lifted up and honored be the name of God,
>made widely known by the example of our graciousness.
Blessed be the name of God, blessed be the Holy One
(though God's graciousness is an inexpressible mystery
>beyond our rendering)
and let us say, Amen.

Pray for your enemy and honor God's way.   Amen.

Unto you gathered here, unto all who teach the ways of God, unto all who listen and live in those Godly ways in this place and in all places, unto them and unto you
>be grief at the fall of God's own,
be transforming love,
be generosity of spirit,
be the study of friendship,
be holy neighborhood,
be prayer for your enemy
>(for your enemy is as fragile as you),
be universal graciousness,
>lived in the presence of God,
and let us say, Amen.

Be like God, gracious and merciful.   Amen.

Love your neighbors and pray for the good of those who curse you.   Amen.

May God who created us all with care
>bless our efforts toward loving peace on earth,
and let us say, Amen.

KADDISH OF QUIET ACTS

Matthew 6:1-13

May God's great name be exalted and sanctified
in this world
made according to God's intentions.
May God govern,
God's redeeming kindness spring forth,
God's Messiah come near and claim us
in your lifetime, in your days,
in the lifetime of all people living today,
and let us say, Amen.

We come to the learning, O Lord. Teach us your ways.   Amen.

Hidden as your God is hidden
shall be your self-discipline.

When you separate yourself from earthly urges
in order to seek God,
adorn yourselves as befits your joyful seeking.
Self-pitying is its own reward.
Your God who is hidden will recognize you.   Amen.

Hidden as your God is hidden
shall be your almsgiving.

When you give of your earthly possessions
in order to seek God,
be unknown.
    Ostentation is its own reward.
Your God who is hidden will recognize you.   Amen.

Hidden as your God is hidden
    shall be your personal prayer.
When you open your heart to speech
    in order to seek God,
      go into a quiet, secret place
    and close the door.
      Gaudy piety is its own reward.
Your God who is hidden will recognize you.   Amen.

When you pray the prayer of your heart,
    pray simply.
God knows you even before you come.
Pray simply, like this,

    Abba,
          let our lives honor your name
          let your home be with us,
          let your ways be our ways,
          let heaven and earth be as one.

          Give us today simply the bread of the morrow.

          Forgive us our violences only as fully
          as we have forgiven others theirs.

          Do not let us stumble,
          give us refuge from evil ways,
          and let us say, Amen.

Know that you are sheltered
        only as you shelter another,
        restored only as you restore another,
        redeemed only as you redeem another,
        and let us say, Amen.

With these teachings, O Lord, may we make your earth holy.   Amen.

Honored be God's name
        (though God be beyond all honors
            humankind can bestow)
        and let us say, Amen.

Unto you who give alms, who fast and who pray, unto all people who
teach others to pray, unto all disciples of prayer, in this place and in all
places, unto you and unto them
        be gentle gifts,
        be closeness to God,
        be holy recognition,
        be comfort,
        be forgiveness as you forgive,
        be many opportunities for quiet deeds,
        be yearning for closeness to YHWH,
        be long life in the presence of our God
            who makes a holy home with us,
        and let us say, Amen.

God forgive us as we forgive.   Amen.

Yours, O God, is the place, the power and the wonder of peace,
                        now and forever.   Amen.

KADDISH OF THE NARROW WAY

Matthew 5:39-42

Gentle and Wisdom is the name of YHWH.
    This earth was created with hope-filled hands.
May we live wisely as God intended,
    with gentleness,
    today, tomorrow and in all times,
and let us say, Amen.

We come to the learning, O Lord. Teach us your ways.   Amen.

Evil resides in this world.
Subdue evil with integrity.
Disarm your enemy with active love.

When your foe lashes out unjustly,
    remain whole.
When you are humiliated,
    let your calm speak its peace.
When you are struck on the face in contempt,
    turn, turn
        in hope that the hater will turn also.   Amen.

Evil is real.
Meet evil with wisdom.
Reach out to the one in whom evil resides.

When your oppressor lays too heavy burdens upon you,
    strengthen yourselves with the lifting of them.
    Remember your ancestors in Egypt,
        how they grew strong,
        how they bonded together,
        how they rose up claiming their God-given freedom.
    Use your burdens for building your bridges to peace.   Amen.

Evil inhabits the weakened heart.
Confront evil with courage.
Rescue your foe from its grip.
When those in authority over you
    force you to go one mile,
        go with them two.
    It is in the shoulder-to-shoulder of walking,
      in the sweat of a well-walked mile,
    that two may bend their heads and talk,
    that one may sway the other,
    that one may draw the other into dialogue.
  Peaceful walking is one small step toward freedom.   Amen.

Evil thrives in greedy living.
Disregard its wily ways.
Embrace the neighbor in its clutches.

When others lust for your possessions,
    meet their jealousy with generous ways,
    transform their covetousness with giving,
    heal twisted hearts with open hands.   Amen.

With these teachings, O Lord, may we make your earth holy.   Amen.

May our thoughtful and courageous living, our attention to an active,
laboring love, our belief in the basic good of every living being, discredit
evil and reflect your way, O God, cause of causes, way of every way
    (though God's disarming love can turn a heart of stone to flesh)
      and let us say, Amen.

Reach out to the one in whom evil resides.   Amen.

Unto all who teach the narrow way, to all who strive to walk it, and
to their companions, to all who are inclined toward evil ways, to all who
seek to turn from them and live, in this time and in all other times
    be quiet wholeness,
    be calm speaking,
    be wisdom,
    be strength,
    be bondedness with others,
    be rising up and claiming,
    be long walks and careful talking,
    be open-handedness and healing generosity,
    be victory over evil ways,
      and let us say, Amen.

Turn, turn in hope that your enemy will turn with you.   Amen.

Raised up in dignity is God's peaceful pathway.   Amen.

Yes, raised up in dignity is my horn of declaring.
My mouth speaks with strength regarding those who do evil to me.
    I am strong because I am secure in my redeeming.   Amen.

May God who desires not the death of the wicked,

may God who desires the wicked to turn and live
    teach us gentle wisdom,
    strengthen us for the building of peace,
    accompany us upon the narrow way,
      and let us say, Amen.

Part Three:
Miryam's Sabbath

Listen,
   the shofar sounds
      from the city the signal sound of the first call.
Awake yourselves,
     the day of difference is at hand.
Ignite your heart.
     The shofar beckons.
     The work of the six days is ended.
     The sabbath approaches.
Come, quickly, come.
     Rest begins.

Clutching one another,
  we still our minds.

O God, help us
   remember who we are . . . children of the Loving One,
   recalling obedience,
   attending to the sabbath.
Six days have we labored, our work is done.
Now on this seventh day,
   the sabbath of the Lord our God,
   we rest in God.
Six days did God labor creating;
   the seventh day God rested.

We, God's image, rest also.

Out of bondedness in Egypt God rescued us
     with a strong hand,
     an outstretched arm,
     so that we might live as God's people.
     You shall keep my sabbath
     that you may know who I am.
     I will make you holy.

PREPARATION

Today we rest from our laboring,
   trusting in God.
Today we rest,
  trusting in God
    who restores us.

Come, quickly.
  Walking together,
    praying together, we retrace the stony path.

Thus says the Lord:

    Keep to the ways of justice
      and do what is good,
      for I am coming.
    My gifts will soon be revealed.
    Blessed is the observant one,
      the child of my heart who is steadfast,
      who keeps the sabbath holy,
      whose hands refrain from evil ways.

How fair are your tents, O Jacob,
    your dwelling place, O Israel.

(The stones are slippery beneath my feet.)

O Lord, I do love abiding in your house;
    by your graciousness do I enter in.

(The stones are slippery beneath my feet.)

Let my prayer come before you, Lord,
    Hearken to me.
    God, in your kindness,
       answer me with truth.

(The stones are slippery
    but my feet step with firmness.
The slippery stones bruise me
    and still I walk secure.)

Solomon's song is my comforting.

I who live must carry on.

    Whither is thy beloved gone
      O thou fairest among women?
    Whither is thy beloved turned aside?

    Where do you pasture?
    Where do you make your flock to rest
      this eventide?

    Return, O return
      that I may look upon thee.

Listen,
    the shofar sounds the second call,
    shops close,
    work turns sabbath-ward.

We've come home.
Friends who have been here preparing
    clasp us close,

enfold us, aching.
Friends who spent the day preparing
    listen,
       absorbing the pain,
       gentling the sorrow.
Friends who have waited the day here
    tend to us lovingly,
    stained garments
       removed, and quickly set to soak.
Nothing is asked of us now.
No one says, "Be still,
          be still, it will be better tomorrow."
No one looks uncomfortably aside.

I pour myself into the mourning,
    awash in the floodtide of grief,
    drowning . . . almost, it seems,
    gathered . . . held to the breast of a friend,
      one of the loved ones
        who waited here today, preparing.

Mourning sounds grow quiet,
    soothed in salving caresses.
      Lo, the sabbath comes.
    Gentled into awareness,
      leaning into those who are there,
      my spirit returns.
Caring touches summon peace.

Ritual observance calls me to holy wakefulness.
    Hands and feet washed,
      cleaned according to our way,
    hair washed and carefully combed through,
    dressed in a clean linen day dress,
      my body is prepared for the day of God.

Some of our company return from the waters,
      sabbath cleansed in mikvah
         at the Mount of Olives pool.
We will go there . . . it is near and quiet.
      The pool of Siloam at the temple gate
         is crowded often at this hour,
            late on the sixth-day eve.

Long shadows of the afternoon are comforting;
      spring breezes on my still damp hair are cool,
      quickened air belying the still heavy
         hot reality of noon.

My arms ache from the weight of him,
      it was just for a moment's time.
      They left me alone,
      holding him there,
      alone for one kind moment,
      his body resting, finally resting
      heavy on my knees,
         strange, bewildering shalom,
      but time was short . . . the sun on its downward course.

I watched them wrap him tenderly,
      entwining his body in clean linen,
      swaddled as I once swaddled his infant frame,
      enwrapped as he daily wrapped himself in his shawl of prayer,
        from heaven to earth . . . from earth to heaven . . .
         born and born and born again,
      light of God wrapped in flickering mystery.

They worked quickly,
      wiping him only,
      leaving the washing till after,
      closing his eyes . . . dabbing with myrrh,

sweet-oil soothing his brow,
    the work as much a gift for them as for him.
      God's law is kind and caring.

We didn't speak aloud,
    hushed the simple prayer and blessings,
    soft-whispered phrases plaintive on the wind,
    resonant the ancient melodies,
    barely audible the sighs.
His head cradled in the resting stone,
    I covered his face with a linen cloth.

Some will return after the sabbath
    to prepare his body in Israel's way,
    but the sun descends, descends,
      and we must hasten now.

The cave where we laid him was cool and clean,
    a womb of healing silence.
It was a relief to leave him there in the quiet,
    safe,
    watched over by God alone.

I sat on the ledge beside him,
    sharing his newly hewn stone,
    solid stone, beneath us both.
      The world stopped . . . finally peaceful,
    scent of fresh linen and sweet-oil
      overcoming the smell of the wood
        and nails and blood and dust and thornspray,
    sound of silence
      drowning out the tumult of the day.

Thought by thought I let it go,
    step by step I put the questioning behind me.

Nearing the Mount of Olives pool,
releasing each haunting memory,
I prepare my mind for God.

Women and men in our little band
    part at the portico of the mikvah,
    stopping for prayer,
    going into the waters clean of body,
        clean of mind.

Slipping out of my day-linen covering,
    I place myself in kindly hands,
        carefully my hair combed through again,
            carefully hands and feet cleansed from the journey.

Hearing the benedictions of those before me,
    I am drawn on.

        Create in me a clean spirit, O God.
        Cleanse my soul.
        Make me ready to abide in your house.

I wade into the water,
    steadied by caring hands.

Welcoming waters!
    Bending my knees, I immerse myself in the flowing pool,
        water closing over my head,
            healed in the watery silence.

        Blessed are you, Adonai, Eloheinu sovereign forever . . .

Prayer, sweet in my mouth,
    again I bend,
        hair floating above me,

stone floor smooth, firm beneath my feet.

Blessed are you, O God, our God,
who has called us to be holy of heart.

Prayer, cleansing on my lips,
once again bending into the waters.

Blessed are you, O God, our God,
Caring Wisdom, Loving Creator
who has called us to be holy of heart
and has taught us the ways of mikvah.   Amen.

Clean of spirit,
step by solid step,
mounting the firm hewn staircase,
the water rushes from me.
Clean of spirit,
standing still,
leaning clean against the careful stones,
loving hands wrap soft rough toweling round my shoulders,
but I prefer the healing breeze,
balm of evening,
to dry me.

I have left behind six days of striving,
entering the seventh day reborn.
I have left behind the touch of death,
readying my soul for the day of God.

Quiet, clothed in sabbath weave and textures,
our company walks the homeward way in peace,
walks in companionship and loving covenant,
walks together from the Mount of Olives
through the Jerusalem roads returning home.

Sunset

Listen,
    the shofar sounds its clarion call;
        as the sun hastens its journey,
        as the stars rush to the festival of evening,
        we come to the sabbath lighting.
Gathered in one room, together we come,
    dispelling the encroaching darkness,
    striking a holy flame,
    lighting the portals of heaven.

And veiling myself,
    I lift my prayer shawl,
        wrapping myself in God;
        the silence is warm and welcoming.
I am caressed in soft wool,
    wound in woven strands of my tradition,
    wound in woven texture of my faith.

        Draw me after you
            let us run.
        Bring me to your chambers.

Praying, I ready myself to light the sabbath lamps,
    I steady myself to step into the light.
Praying, I strive with the darkness.

        My soul magnifies the Lord
           and my spirit lifts itself in your presence.
        O God, my God,
           you stand watch over me.

Age upon age you draw me into the shelter of your wing
and I am comforted.
O God, my God,
    you walk with us.
        Age upon age your footsteps reverberate in the mountains,
            the valleys are aroused,
                we your people are awakened.

    Holy is your name.
    You shake us in the darkness.
        In the midst of turbulence
        you are peace.
    You pity us in our laboring.
        In the turmoil of striving
        you are rest.
O God, my God,
        you summon us.
        Age upon age you sound your bewildering call.
        Age upon age we answer you,
            stumbling we dance,
            stuttering we raise our song,
            quaking we strike the flame,
                lighting the darkness
                    with your promised holiness.

Merciful Lord, bless us, your family.
Come dwell among us today.

God, only God,
        I come to kindle the lamps.
        I come to begin the sabbath.
Your prophet Isaiah said to us:
        If you hold back your foot from trampling on the sabbath,
        indeed if you keep yourself for me on my day,

if you call the sabbath delightful
and the holy day of the Lord honorable,
if you fill the day with graciousness,
then shall you find peace in YHWH,
then shall I lift you up from despair,
then shall I bring you to the mountain,
feeding you with your heritage.
I will care for you.

Merciful Lord, bless us, your family.
Come dwell among us today,
make us worthy to teach your ways,
worthy to raise up your children in holiness.
Hear our prayer, O Lord,
let our cry come near to you.
Hide not from us in these days,
hearken to our calling,
come with haste.

Those who dwell in darkness cannot reflect your light.
I light the lamps in blessing,
one in vigilance,
one in remembering.

Blessed are you, our Lord, governor of heaven and earth:
You have sanctified us with your teachings.
You have taught us to kindle the sabbath lamps.   Amen.

May our home be made holy with these lights.
Here we serve you with awe
as in the days of old.
May our offering of this day be pleasing to you.

The gifts of the lamps warm my cheeks
and illumine the eyes of those of us gathered.

107

Holy gifts of warmth and light.

Gift the palms of my hands with your treasures
     as I draw near to you.
Warmed,
     lightened,
     I rest.
Silenced,
     resting in the palm of God's hand,
     broken, I rest.

     Whither is my beloved gone?

     Return, O return
     that we may look upon thee.

     O daughters of Jerusalem,
       I beg you stir not
         nor waken my love
         until my love pleases.

     Beloved, set me as a seal upon your heart,
       for my love is strong as death.

I lift my face and the light beckons.
Surely this is peace,
     surely this God's rest,
     a house lit with holy lamps,
     a home filled with the light of friends.

Now, the prayer of women, Hannah's prayer:
Reaching back into the hearts of women of old,
     I draw the covering of prayer over us.

My heart is full in YHWH,
raised up in dignity is my horn of praising.
My mouth speaks with strength
   regarding those who do evil toward me
     because I am secure in my redeeming.

There is none holy as YHWH is holy,
   indeed, none beside our God.
Nor is there any other rock like God.

Speak neither with boasting
   nor arrogance.
Our God is mindful,
   acting with fairness.
The weapons of the mighty are useless,
   and they that stumble are strengthened.

Those who were filled
   hire themselves out for bread,
   while the hungry are fed to fatness.
The childless bears seven children;
   the mother of many is bereft.

YHWH gives death.
YHWH gives life.
YHWH accompanies the dead into the grave
   and brings them out again.
YHWH makes poverty and riches,
      brings low and lifts up,
       raises the poor from the dust and
       lifts the beggar from the debris.
YHWH seats the lowly beside the noble ones.
The foundation stones of the world are God's;
   upon them is the universe set firm.
The Lord guards the footpath of the faithful;

the unfaithful walk their way in darkness,
    unable to survive on their own resources.
It is YHWH who shatters disbelief,
    indeed thunders upon hard-heartedness.
The Lord, our God,
    will measure the span of our days,
    will strengthen the anointed,
    will raise up in exultation the horn of the chosen.   Amen.

I gaze upon my home lit by the sabbath lamps,
    and I know my tent is at peace.
I come to my dwelling place
    and all is secure.
The peace of God is summoned only by light,
    for God saw the light
        that it was good.

Come, my beloved companions.
    May the healing radiance of the sabbath shine forth in our hearts.
    The Lord is our light and our salvation.
    Let us welcome the sabbath.

Our embracing is gentle and deep,
    our voices soft between us,
    whispering the sabbath greeting of peace.

    Shabbath shalom.

Evening Prayer

Listen,
     the shofar sounds its final call;
     three clear notes and
     ma'ariv, evening prayer, begins.

YHWH summons us:
     Come, I will whisper to you quietly,
       for the sabbath walks on light feet toward you.
     Veiled she approaches, glowing and scented.
     As the night falls she accompanies you.

     Beloved, come let us meet the bride.
     Blessed is the bride, the sabbath moment.
       She is in our care.
       Love her, beloved.
       Love her dearly.

     Come, taste how good it is on the mountain.

     Come, let us sing.
     Our Rock awaits us.

     Come, let us attend with softened hearts.
     YHWH, our Creator, is present.
     This is our God.
     We are the people of the holy pasture.
     We are the flock guided by the loving shepherd.

Planted in the vineyard of YHWH,
we will bear fruit.
The holy hand alone will harvest us.

It is good to give thanks to YHWH,   *Psalm 92*
    to sing in honor of your name, Most High,
    to tell of your tenderness in the dawning
    and of your faith in the darkest hour.

Upon the ten-stringed instrument
    our gentle hallelujahs surge;
    our still voice of blessing rises on the breeze.
Your wonders are the theme of my song,
    in the works of your hands my victory.

How brilliant your work, YHWH.
How deep your purposes.

The unknowing do not see this,
    nor do the shallow understand.

When the thoughtless bloom
    and the careless blossom,
    they will fade quickly.
But you flourish forever.
Behold, Adonai,
    how those who disregard you falter.

My horn of praising is raised up in dignity,
    with ever-fresh oil am I anointed.

My eyes have seen the fate of my foes,
    my ears have heard of their defeat.

Those who know you will be fruitful as the date palm,

hardy as the cedars in Lebanon.
Planted in YHWH's vineyard,
   rooted in the garden of God,
   they will bear fruit even into old age.
Vigorous and youthful they will be,
   declaring YHWH is just and merciful,
   the rock in whom there is no faltering.   Amen.

YHWH reigns upon the throne of everlasting   *Psalm 93*
    graciousness.
   God has donned garments of wonder,
   has put on the gown of knowledge.
The Lord has set firm the universe
   and it will not be shaken.

Your sovereign power has been from the beginning.
You are forever.

The turbulent waters have broken loose, O Lord,
   thrashing floods have pounded our shores.
Stronger than tidal waves you remain,
   steadfast you stand upon the mountain.

Your ways are trustworthy, sturdy your house,
   holiness is your dwelling place.
O Lord,
   I know you are the everlasting one.   Amen.

The voice of YHWH summons us,   *Psalm 29*
   stirs the cedar;
   indeed the cedar of Lebanon stirs with strength.
The voice of YHWH sets the wilderness a-shaking,
   even the wilderness deep within us shatters and quakes.
The voice of YHWH hones the lightning,

even the shafts of light from heaven's home are sharpened.

YHWH sits enthroned,
     mighty in the midst of creation.
YHWH gives strength to us.
YHWH blesses us with peace.   Amen.

We come to the oldest of the old, the singing of the Shema.
     In all times we have stood as a people
     in grief and in pleasure.
     In wilderness and in homeland,
     from Sinai unto Jerusalem,
          our cry has come as you have commanded.

     Blessed are you, our God sovereign of the universe.
     You speak and evening begins.
     You set the seasons to pulsing,
          the heavens to their graceful dance.
     You create night and day.
     Light and darkness you set in perpetual rhythm,
          passing before us, dividing and foreshadowing.
     Blessed are you
          who speaks and evening begins.   Amen.

     You, YHWH, have loved us with an everlasting love,
          we who have found pardon in the wilderness
               and have survived the lure of the sword.
     We go to our rest.

     YHWH has appeared to us from afar saying,

          I have loved you with unwavering tenderness.
          I am constant in my affection for you.

You have taught us.
>   Your teachings are our life and the length of our days.
>   We will meditate upon them
>   at our lying down and at our rising.

>   We will plant and gather.
>   In you we shall be gathered,
>   a great company returning by a smooth path,
>   not stumbling.
>   Blessed are you, YHWH,
>   you who have loved us with a great and everlasting love.   Amen.

Sitting, we enter your silence;
>   stilling ourselves, we prepare.

>   Draw me after you
>   Bring me to your chambers.

Resting, eyes covered in the palm of our right hand,
>   we enter your pasture.

>   Draw me after you
>   Bring me to your chambers.

Attending, hearts reaching for you,
>   we enter your holy place, singing,

>   Shema Israel
>   Adonai Eloheinu
>   Adonai echod.

Listening, we speak the ancient revelation:

>   Hear, Israel.

The Lord is your God.
The Lord alone.

Blessed is the name of God forever.   Amen.

Listening, we speak the ancient invitation:

Love YHWH with all your heart,
    with all your mind,
    with all your strength.
Write these words upon your heart.
Say them over and over to your children;
    say them at rest or walking abroad,
    at your lying down and at your rising.
Fasten them on your arm as a sign and
    let them be as a mark between your eyes.
Inscribe them on the doorposts of your house
    and on your gates.   Amen.

We rise for the Amidah prayer.
All Israel stands.
Three times each day Israel stands before the Lord.
On this day, on the sabbath
    we stand for joy.
There is no guilt or despairing on the sabbath.

We walk.
All Israel walks.
Three steps forward Israel climbs the mountain of the Lord.
With Moses, our rabbi, we ascend the holy mountain
    where God hearkens to our prayer.

O Lord, open thou my lips and my mouth shall praise you.

O Lord, our God, and God of those who have gone before us:
God of Abraham and Sarah,
God of Isaac and Rebecca,
God of Jacob and Leah and Rachel,
God who sustains us,
God who remembers good things,
    in you is oneness from the beginning unto the present time,
    from the present time into the world to come.
Blessed are you,
    Shield of the ancient spark of Abraham and Sarah
    living in us today.   Amen.

O Lord who saves,
who sustains the living with loving kindness,
who revives the dead with great mercy,
who lifts up the fallen,
        heals the sick,
        loosens the bound,
        keeps faith with those asleep in the dust.
Who is like you, O God?
In you is the call to life.
In you is the call to death.
In you is the call to everlasting love.
Blessed are you, Adonai,
    who keeps faith with your people.   Amen.

Holy, Holy, Holy,
the earth is full of your glory.
Blessed are you.

God of Israel,
you did hallow the seventh day.
Accept our rest.
May we be holy in your teachings.
Gladden us.

Purify our hearts to serve you in truth.
We are favored, Lord, in the inheritance of the sabbath.
We will care for her today and always.   Amen.

Blessed are you, our God, restorer of faith.
May our service give you pleasure:
    As we do on earth
    so is it done in heaven.

Your wonders grace our moments.
Your care for us is eternal.

May peace be our harvest
    in our homes and palaces, peace.   Amen.

May the words of my mouth and the meditation of my mind
    find favor before you, God, my rock and my redeemer.   Amen.

Our prayer of the sabbath evening draws to an end.
There is comfort for us in the ancient and the common words.

Blessed are you, Beloved,
    who gives us the sabbath bride.

God is our shield in whom the dead are revived.
There is no one beside the Holy One.
God gives rest to us on the sabbath,
    reviving rest to a faithful people.

YHWH summons us to a sabbath table.
    Water and wine,
    bread and salt,
    light and love await us there.
Come, my companions,
    sorrow is for another day,

for YHWH has spoken.

The sabbath I give over to you,
   not you to the sabbath.
This day shall be not your burden but your delight.
Take care of her.
Treasure her that she be ever pleasured.

Gathering around the table,
   the holy altar of our home,
   we pour the wine and bless it.

   Blessed are you, Adonai,
     sovereign of the universe,
     creator of the fruit of the vine. Amen.

We pass the simple bowl of water and the napkin,
   each one offering hands and help along the way,
   washing, praying, watching,
   attending to the ritual we love.

Clean spirits rest their hands upon the bread to bless it,
   lingering awhile over the bread and wine and prayer,
   tasting the goodness of God's ways.
The food is rich and nourishing,
   lovingly prepared by friends who stayed behind today.
The talk is soft and comforting;
   there is no place this night for hardness.
Cherishing Torah thoughts,
   comforting our God in a world
     where too many gather at tables seasoned with idle chatter,
      shuddering with disharmony,
     where too many are discontented and forgetful.
Cherishing Torah thoughts, we speak of God's ways:

the mystery of this day,
    comforting hope
        and our intention that this day will be lived in our truth,
    our sabbath day of honor and God's pleasure.

Slowly the melodies begin,
    soft, ancient songs
    sabbath table hallowing.

    Run Beloved run.
        Draw near to our chamber of sabbath
            where our intent this night is for loving.

GRACE AFTER MEALS: BIRKA'AT HAMAZON

It is for those who have eaten together, to pray together.
It is for those who have eaten of God's own, to give thanks.
  God is our rock,
    our sustenance,
    from whose storehouse all good things come.

When the Lord restored the freedom of Zion   *Psalm 126*
  we were like unto them that dream.
Then was our mouth filled with laughter,
  and they said among the nations,
    The Lord has done great things for them.

Indeed, the Lord has done great things for us.
Turn us again, O Lord.
They that sow in tears shall reap in joy.
Though they go their way weeping,
  leaving a trail of fertile seeds,
  they shall return singing
  bringing in the sheaves.   Amen.

Blessed are you, our God.   *From Moses*
You provide for our needs in the desert;
  you have given us bread for this day.
We are grateful.

121

Your heritage is a good land.   *From Joshua*
    Your desire is a fruitful earth.
You teach us freedom and kindness
    in every hour, in every day, in every season.

Sustain Jerusalem, your resting place.   *From David*
Restore the house of David, the anointed one.   *and*
Secure Jerusalem in our labor.   *Solomon*
    Let us tend, nourish, sustain, support.
    Let us relieve burdens that are too heavy.
    Let us work, harvest, prepare and distribute
        as you have commanded us,
        in steadfast toil, joy and generosity
        as befits a people of God.
May we come to you that seventh day
    in precious rest and refreshment.
Blessed are you
    who teaches us care of the land and its people.   Amen.

Those who make the table of God their eating place
        will be content.
Those who sit at the table of greed
        will never be satisfied.
Trust in the Merciful One.
Only God is enough.
Blessed be God forever.   Amen.

The lights flicker on,
        the wicks fueled by the remaining oil.
We will keep watch upon this holy evening
        until they fade.
Sitting round the table still,
        though several have stirred themselves,

one stands by the east window.
Israel's sabbath lights shine from many windows.
Jewish homes spill out their faith into the darkness.
Jerusalem lives tonight.

Whither is my beloved gone?
   The watcher that goes about the city found me,
     to whom I said,
       Saw ye the one whom my soul loves?

   Return, return
     that we may look upon thee.

I charge you, O daughters of Jerusalem,
   that you stir not up
   nor awake my love
   until my love pleases.

We speak together of other sabbath times.
   Tonight, this sabbath,
   we rest in God.
Gentle stories spill out into the night.
   Tonight, this sabbath,
   we heal. God reaches out.
Laughter,
   my God, how beautiful.
   Tonight, this sabbath,
   we laugh. God reminds us of the softer times.

   I am the rose of Sharon,
     the lily of the valley.
   You, my beloved,
     the blossom among the thorns.

You, my beloved,
    the fruitful bush in the wildwood.
I am comforted in your shade.
You have brought me into your generous house.
Your intent toward me is for love.

The company drifts toward evening's rest.
Some to the peace of an evening walk,
    others to the sleeping mat.

    Tell me
        O thou whom my soul loves,
    Where are your pastures?
    Where do you make your flock to rest at eventide?

By night upon my mat
I seek him whom my soul loves.
I seek him and find him not.

I sleep but my heart wakes.
    The voice of my beloved knocks at my heart.
    Open, open to me,
        my love, my precious one.

O, daughters of Jerusalem,
    I charge you stir not
        nor wake my love
            until my love pleases.

Sabbath Day

This is the sabbath of God.

This is the day the Lord has made holy,
　　we will rejoice and be glad in it.

This is the day of days,
　　setting aside from the other six,
　　looking away from our labors and distress,
　　declaring that God is kind and life is good.

Wakening we greet the day, sign of our covenant.
　　Blessed the One who gives rest to the people Israel.

Washing and dressing we go quickly to prayer.
　　Blessed the One who calls the people to gather.

Singing we sink into the sabbath rhythms.
　　Blessed the One who creates the praises of Judah.

Nishmat, prayer of sabbath morning,
　　how lovely it feels in my mouth.

　　The breath of every being shall bless your name, Lord our God,
　　　　and the spirit of all flesh shall witness to your presence.
　　In this world and in the world to come, you are God.

　　There is none beside you,
　　　　none other to redeem,
　　　　none other to save.

There is none other to set us free,
　　none other to support us.
Indeed, there is none other to have mercy
　　in times of trouble and anguish.

Yes, truly yes,
　　we have no one but you.
You are God of the first and the last
　　guiding the world with loving kindness
　　and your creatures with mercy.
You, Lord, neither slumber nor sleep.
You rouse the sleeper to thoughtfulness
　　and awaken those who slumber to examine their ways.
You give words to the speechless
　　and loosen the bound.
You lift up the fallen
　　and lighten the burdened.

To you alone do we give thanks.

If our mouth were as full of song as the sea,
　　our tongue as full of merriment as the waves,
　　our lips as full of praise as the breadth of the sky,
If our eyes shone like the sun and moon,
　　our hands outspread like eagles on the wing,
　　our feet as swift as hinds,
Lo, even these would not be enough to express our gratitude
　　for thousands upon thousands upon thousands
　　　　of gracious gifts you have given us
　　　　　　throughout our generations.

You brought us out from bondedness,
　　you, our redeemer.

In hunger, you nourish us,

in violence you are there beside us, rescuing.
From enduring disease you deliver us.
Until now your mercy has helped us,
    your loving kindness has not left us.

O God, our God, do not abandon us.

All that is within us,
    life and limb,
    spirit and soul,
    tongue and speech stand ready.
Behold, here am I, prepared,
    blessing your holy name.
To you every mouth shall sing,
    every tongue pledge faithfulness,
    every knee shall bend,
    every body will bow down.
All hearts shall adore you,
    innermost thoughts and feelings
    radiate your wonders.
As it is written:
    All my bones shall say,
    Lord, who is like you?

You deliver the poor from those stronger than they,
    the needy from those who rob them.
Who is like you, O Lord?
    Who is equal? Who can compare?
You are the One Alone!

Bless the Lord, O my soul,
    let all that is within me bless God's holy name.   Amen.

Long and quiet are the sabbath mornings deep in prayer and learning.

In common we gather, sharing who we are,
    pleasuring our adoring God,
    gifting as we have been gifted with a presence.

After prayer and eating
    we fill the time with generosity.
Study, sometimes
    quiet talking,
    and of course the children.
        They share their thoughts, we speak of heartfelt things.
          This is the day we teach and listen with the children.
          Today is the day we live in the place of God.
Walking, quiet ones upon the pathway,

    Be not vengeful, says the Lord, but love them all.

Touching, gentle comfort as we pass each other,
    trusting in the Lord and doing good,
    dwelling in the land and cherishing faithfulness,
    making YHWH the source of our peace.
Tempted by the sweep of fear and thoughts of vacant days ahead,
    lured by the inclination to respond with blood,
    we resist—we help each other to resist.
        Our beings centered in resistance,
          we refuse the lesser way.

O God, may no one be punished for what has been done to us.
    The age-old prayers sustain.
O God, may no one suffer in our cause.

We will rise up according to the Master's way, becoming
    flourishing again.

This day is for YHWH's rest.
    In it we commit our way to YHWH's way.

Trust and the path will open.
Enough of rage . . . leave vengeance aside.
Repay evil with love.
Hold on only a little longer now
    and the kindly ones come into their own.
Gentle as doves,
        wise as serpents, we continue,
        pressing on God's way.

HAVDALAH

It is evening.
It is the coming out of the sabbath.

    Behold, my God is my rock.
    I have trust now.
    I have laid aside my fear.
    YHWH is my strength and my song.
    Confident, I draw water from the saving springs.
    In our midst is the Holy One.
    Lifting the saving cup,
       I call upon the name of my God.

    Blessed are you, our God, master from everlasting to everlasting
    who creates the fruit of the vine.   Amen.

Smelling the fragrant sabbath spices,
    continue the lively scent of sabbath delight
        through the days to come.
Feeling the warmth on your hands of the firelight,
    sustain the sabbath flame
        for six long days until we come again to sabbath.
  Blessed fire, inspire our coming days,
    transform darkness to light,
          cold to warmth,
          grain to bread,
          metal to tools,
          loneliness to companionship.
  Blessed are you, Lord our God.

Listen, all of us to the honor of YHWH,
   distinguish between the holy and unholy,
   between substance and shadow,
   between faith and fruitless fervor.
Blessed are you,
   who teaches us to know the difference
   and act with integrity.

The bride passes from us.
Taste wine with me,
      carry sabbath peace into tomorrow.
Spill a bit of wine in sorrow for her passing.

The bride passes from us.
   In her presence we have rested.
   Kindled and cared for we take up the work of the earth,
      dwelling with one heart in peace.
   Slowly she leaves us as night settles in.
   Extinguish her flame.
   Carry on.
   Alleluia.   Amen.

The sun sets on our sabbath.

And It Was Evening, and It Was Morning of the First Day

The sun has set upon the sabbath.

It is the evening of the first day.

I sing from Solomon's song.
I who live, carry on.

> Tell me,
>   O thou whom my soul loves,
>   Where do you pasture?
>   Where do you make your flock to rest
>   at morning tide?
>
> I sleep, but my heart wakes.
> The voice of my beloved knocks at my heart.
> Open, open to me, my precious one.

Soon it will be morning,
    the first day.

Soon some will go to the garden,
    gathering myrrh with spice.
Soon,

    Return, O return
        that we may look upon thee.

It is gray,
    the frivolity of first light
    that drives away all but the morning star.
The deep darkness that follows before dawn
    will shelter them in their journey.
There is much to carry
    both in the heart and hand,
    but the way is sure.
In the tent of YHWH is peace
    in the work of the coming morning,
    for thy law is a light on our pathway.
We lean into each other
    before the leaving,
    in our embrace, security,
    in our murmurings, faithful love.

    My shepherd is the Lord,   *Psalm 23*
        there is nothing I shall want.
    In the Lord I rest,
        fragrant pastures my resting place.
    In you I am restored,
        still waters my abode.
    My redeemer rescues my soul,
        living deserts my home.
    Yes, the Lord cares for me.
        When I walk in the shadow of death
        I am not afraid.
    You, my sustainer, are there.

Quieting me,
    thy rod measures me compassionately.
Lifting me up,
    thy Torah supports me gently.
You are my comfort.
You prepare my table even in the midst
        of those that do violence to me;
        even there in the darkest suffering,
    I discover holy food.
    I feel the touch of soothing oil on my head,
        my cup of life is full to overflowing.
Whatever follows in the days of my life,
    your goodness,
    your mercy will accompany me.
You are my dwelling place,
    my home forever.   Amen.

Bidding them a fruitful journey,
    I am alone again.

    It is the morning of the first day.

    I charge you,
        O daughters of Jerusalem,
        that you stir not
        nor wake my love
        until my love pleases.

    I am the rose of Sharon,
        the lily of the valleys.
    You, my beloved,
        the blossom among the thorns.
    You, my beloved,

the fruitful bush upon the mountainside.
I am enlivened in your shadow.
You have brought me into your generous house.
Your intent toward me is for love.

Hark, my love.
The voice of my beloved.

Behold,
   he comes!
Like one leaping upon the mountains.
Like one skipping upon the hills.

My beloved spoke
   and said to me,
     Rise up, my love, my fair one,
      and come away.
For, lo, the winter is past,
   the rain is over and gone.
The blossom buds forth upon the earth.
     The time of pruning has come.
     The voice of the turtle is heard in our land.
     The fig tree ripens with fruit.
     The fruit of the vine is fragrant.

Arise, my love,
     my fair one,
       and come.

EPILOGUE:
REFLECTIONS
OF A RABBI

A Journey in Holiness

Miryam's challenge is unequivocal, a call for a Jewish-Christian reconciliation, a call for the cleansing of a pain-filled past. It is a time for renewal,

> reaching always for the best in both of us,
> for it is in our sacred dreams,
> our lifted vision of ourselves in God,
> that rests the journey home.

The "best in both of us" would have us love one another as neighbors, as ourselves. The "sacred dream" would have us love the Lord, our God, with all our heart, with all our soul, with all our might. The "vision" is where history is grounded in hope, God its intent. The "journey home" finds us resting as sisters and brothers in God's holy presence, hallowing the earth by that which is done and thereby being hallowed ourselves.

Miryam of Judah is the story of a journey. Miryam, lovingly researched and caringly etched by Ann Johnson, is a journeyer. She journeys as a daughter of Judah. She journeys as a woman, as a mother. She journeys as a Jew. And, all the while, her journey is a journey cupped in holiness.

————————

Miryam journeys as a daughter of Judah, saying,

Be like your God, . . .
  for you are created in the holy image

Be the name of God, blessed be the Holy One
  (though God's graciousness is an inexpressible mystery beyond our rendering).

May God's will be done on earth as in heaven.

What I do on earth so it is done in heaven. . . .
Let heaven and earth be as one.

But this is easier said than done. After all, God is experienced as both far away and close at hand, transcendent and immanent. How does one take that sublime holiness, that divine perfection, and image it in this world?

Miryam's answer is really quite simple. The Jewish people are called to learning, to prayer and to deeds of kindness:

Learning. Picture a community whose commandment it was to learn at home or when walking abroad, when retiring or when arising . . . always an intense grasping to walk with God, to befriend God, to rest in God's holiness.

Judaism learns of God's holiness (kedushah) as being the fullness of all ethical qualities. Not only is the Leviticus passage "You shall be holy; for I the Lord your God am holy" central to this tradition, but God's most common name was and is "The Holy One, blessed be the One" (Ha'Kadosh Baruch Hu). This holiness is transcendent, a self-contained perfection beauteous in its sublimeness. But, at the same time, this holiness is imminent and may be imaged here on earth, providing a life-giving opportunity for kindly, active and fruitful maturation.

In fact, Rabbinic tradition understood God as having provided examples of this holiness in the ancient scriptures, the Torah. A glimpse of one of these shines through Miryam's own life experience at Golgotha (God is depicted as accompanying Moses to his sepulchre, and standing watch). And her son-the-Rabbi's teachings were certainly steeped in this tradition (humility—the Holy One ignored lofty mountains and fine trees when the "Shechinah," God's glory, alighted on the lowly Mount Sinai and the burning bush; compassion—clothing the naked Eve and Adam before their exit from the Garden of Eden; forgiveness—Cain, the world's first condemned murderer, caringly protected with God's mark, lovingly blessed with children who were builders, musicians and artisans). As Miryam herself states it,

> God, blessed be the Holy One,
>   never asks of us that which
>   God, the Holy One,
>   has not first performed.

> God walks where we walk.

> Each of us. . .
>   hallowing this ground, . . .
>   believing . . .
>   that in this simple act of kindness
>   earth is made more kind.

In this way Judah establishes an intimate kinship with the Holy One, also named "Our Father" and "My Beloved."

Judah, then, had been gifted with being an enabler, a hallower of the earth. Companioned by learning, Judah's light was the holy Word, with Torah being its revelation.

With loving deeds and learning, I build a fence around the Torah,
    enclosing thereby a soft, protected, fertile place
        for God and I and all creation,
        thus to thrive and grow.
Be Torah-true. . . .
search out God's heart within each word,
    fill it full with your loving
    and carry on from there.
We will continue faithful,
    observing Torah,
    imaging you.
Never, never, will we let the learning die.

Prayer. Picture a community praying ceaselessly.

Day by day, each morning (shacharit), each afternoon (minchah) and each evening (ma'ariv), the community rested in prayers of praise, petition and thanksgiving. These were prayers bounded by and permeated with a yearning for holiness, the word "kedushah" being ever present.

In addition, moment by moment the individual was readied with innumerable blessings. The blessings were uttered prayerfully, instantaneously and spontaneously, sensual experiences of natural phenomena calling for an acknowledgment of God's presence in the world. Indeed, there was delight in being chosen as a hallower of the world, "Blessed art thou, Adonai, our Lord, sovereign of the universe, who has commanded us to sanctify. . . ."

Moreover, since prayer and learning were regarded as equally experiencing God's presence, it is not surprising that a prayer emerged called "The Rabbis' Kaddish" (Kaddish d'Rabbanan), "kaddish" being a word rooted in holiness. Proclaiming, blessing and praising God as holy, the content, process and dynamic of learning is lived as being holy in God's presence.

Deeds of kindness. Torah-true and lovers of the Law, the daughters and sons of Judah knew that it was theirs to love God by loving their neighbor, and in loving their neighbor they would be loving God. Having a vision of constant learning and prayer, they strove to knead the earth with holy deeds of kindness (hesed). They yearned to image the Holy One's presence both in act and thought. They sanctified God's name (Kiddush Hashem).

And there was the calling to sanctify God's name beyond the requirements of the Torah, the Law. It was akin to a child wishing to please a loving parent before the request, in fact even if the request was not forthcoming. It was a superior state of holiness called saintliness (hasiduth).

Such is the story of Miryam's women of remembrance, daughters of Judah. Bathsheba summons David to a renewal of his covenant regarding Solomon, insuring the succession of a monarch who would image God as compassionate judge. Ruth redeems Naomi, securing her covenant by kin and providing her with a son. Rahab believes without seeing, conversion flowing from full faith. Tamar's tenacity brings Judah back to God. Theirs were deeds of kindness pleasing to God, acts of holiness, saintliness.

————————————

Miryam journeys as a woman and as a mother. Grounded on this earth, the stumbling sandled feet of the last mile are firmed, the surefootedness of a faith reaffirmed.

As woman, accompanied by spiritual sisters linked by the feminine face searching through time, the past becomes inspiration for the present and vision for the future (and not only for women, but enabling men in a deepening of their experience of the masculine face of "lifeing"). Sisters grounded in the sheer delight of one's own sensuality, filled with the fullness of birthing, refreshed and renewed by God's gift of ritual, calling companions to a centeredness in God's holiness.

As mother, deepened by her son's ancestral heritage, enriched by her son as rabbi, as teacher and preacher, Miryam was a companion to him and he to her before and after that last mile. Resting in prayerful reflection and rumination, the pain of a mother's loss heals, and the healed becomes the healer in her mothering of a community huddled, clutching and leaning into one another. The haunting memories having been assuaged, mother and mothered walk in the shadow of death unafraid, both in that generation and in generations to come.

Filled by the fullness of the covenantal cup, she centers herself in a people whose chosenness is to seek holiness by seeding God's presence, living sanctified time. And so it is that this sabbath of sabbaths, resting as it does between darkness and light, is unequivocally demanding in its insistence that grief gives way to delight and sanctification. Thus this daughter of Judah is grounded in trusting certainty that God's sovereignty assures that "It is good!" and that despair, defeat and death are cupped lovingly in hope, triumph and life.

—————————————

Miryam journeys as Jew, companioned by men and women who are Jewish, a son who is Jewish and a covenantal chosenness anchored in Jewishness.

Pope John Paul II, joining the Jewish community in Rome's principal synagogue in April of 1986, stated this succinctly:

> Christians have learned this desire (for love and justice) of the Lord from the Torah, which you venerate, and from Jesus who took to its extreme consequence the love demanded by the Torah. . . .

> The Jews are beloved of God who has called them with an irrevocable calling. . . .

It is a holy moment in history in which sisters and brothers can (must) return home healed, a family warmed by the togetherness of shared experiences, delighted by and respectful of the uniqueness of respective pilgrimages, and nourished by the prospects of a unity in which all will bask in God's holiness on earth as it is in heaven, heaven and earth being as one.

Perry Cohen, Rabbi